THE MAN FROM YUMA

THE MAN FROM YUMA

JOHN HUNTER

SAGEBRUSH
Large Print Westerns

First published in Great Britain by ISIS Publishing Ltd.
First published in the United States by Berkley Books

Published in Large Print 2010 by ISIS Publishing Ltd.,
7 Centremead, Osney Mead, Oxford OX2 0ES
by arrangement with
Golden West Literary Agency

British Library Cataloguing in Publication Data
Hunter, John, 1903–1980.
The man from Yuma.
1. Western stories.
2. Large type books.
I. Title
813.5'2–dc22

ISBN 978–0–7531–8506–3 (hb)

Printed and bound in Great Britain by
T. J. International Ltd., Padstow, Cornwall

CHAPTER
ONE

The stage from Sodaville was full and Emma Bondford had never in her life been so uncomfortable. Nine passengers were packed inside on the three upholstered seats, and another six had clambered on top with the driver.

The heavy Concord lurched with jarring force down the ruts that unreeled across the white alkali fiats of the high Nevada desert, now straight as a taut string from horizon to horizon, now shattered like a broken porcelain rod. It was a thin, unbeautiful road, cut deep into the brittle crust of this wasteland by hundreds of high iron wheels, their sharp impressions unleavened by rain, not softened even by blowing sand; for none blew here. The landscape was rigid. The history of traffic lay bald and undisturbed on the face of the land. It was a busy road, one serpentine line of great freight wagons inching southward, hauling supplies down to Tonopah and the newer Goldfield, a second opposing it, carting heavy loads of ore north up the tortuous miles to meet the narrow gauge railroad that ended at Sodaville. It was an old road, by the calendar of the people who used it, already into its fifth year.

Nevada had had a twenty-year hiatus from such important activity as this. When the mines at Virginia City collapsed, and the tunnels at Tombstone flooded, the mining population dissolved like smoke, dispersing, some to the booming Colorado camps, some to Montana and Idaho, others taking the bitter route to the Alaskan diggings hard by the Arctic Circle, and the southern desert slept.

Now men were swarming back, drawn by the silver deposits at Tonopah and the fresh discoveries of gold further south. Everyone who could afford the fare, could borrow a horse, or could walk, plunged into the bewildering desert on the eastern rim above Death Valley. And no more cruel land exists in the whole west. The white alkali, reflecting the heat of hell, gives way like melting snow to an ancient terrain crisscrossed by rotten lava flows, to mountains of volcanic ash and deep gullies scooped out by flash floods swollen with summer rains in the bleak, barren, heaved-up spines above.

Across the flats the impatient stage made its own third road, free of the wagons. In the broken land it returned to the freighters' trace and the slow crawl, swerved around upthrust rock bursts, dropped into arroyos, jolted heavily over huge black dykes that lay across its path like sleeping reptiles turned to stone.

Emma Bondford was the only woman on the coach. She was a tall girl with fair hair neatly pinned into the crown of her traveling hat, obviously stifling in the ill-advised, high-necked costume. Her blue eyes were puffed from the gritty dust, her lips cracked and sore from the searing dryness of the choking air. She wanted to cry. She had certainly never pictured anything like this when she had agreed to come.

It had sounded like salvation, listening to her father's lawyer in the man's Chicago office, as if God had taken pity on her in her misery and prepared a place for her. She had been penniless, untrained for any kind of employment in business or in a profession, shocked to numb thoughtlessness by the suddenness of her father's suicide. She could forgive him his business failure, but not the act of taking his own life.

"I sent for you," the lawyer said, "because I may have found a solution for you. I have a client in Goldfield, a man who lost his wife six months ago. He has two small children, a boy, a little over seven, a girl, a year younger. He has a housekeeper; but he wants a governess to teach them, give them a background in keeping with their financial status."

"Where is Goldfield? I've never heard of it."

"In Nevada. It's a new mining town and very rich, from all reports. He will pay one hundred and fifty dollars a month and your living."

The lawyer was an old man with thin white hair and a pink scalp shining through. He had known her all of her life and was concerned for her. Now he was proud of the way she straightened, accepting the suggestion.

"Fortunes are being made there," he encouraged. "Amos Frost, my client, is an assayer and very wealthy. He took a million dollars from a mine in Tombstone." He was silent for a moment, considering how to phrase what he wanted to say next, and decided on bluntness.

3

"You are a very attractive young woman, my dear, and I understand that there are not enough ladies in that country."

His meaning was clear enough that her cheeks colored. She did not argue aloud, but her chin lifted proudly. She would not go shopping for a husband because of money. She would go to build her own new life.

But after nearly two days in the agony of the coach she was not as confident that she could survive in this raw land at all. The first day had been bad enough, and the night in the thin-walled hotel room in Tonopah was terrifying. Today was even worse. With the heat and the sour dust she could barely breathe, and the man crowded next to her on the seat was drunk.

He had been drunk when he had climbed aboard at Tonopah, the fumes of whiskey surrounding him like an aura, and if there had been any way she could have moved she would have done so, but there was no place to go. The man on her left was already asleep, and the drunken one began to snore before the coach was a hundred yards from the station.

As long as he slept she supposed that she could bear it; still she looked hopefully at the three figures facing her. The man directly across was white-haired, although he did not appear old. His eyes, a remote, shadowed blue, looked not at her but through her, through the back of the coach, on to the distant receding hills. For a moment they were open, then they dropped, and he let his head fall forward and to all intent joined his neighbors in sleep. It seemed to her that everyone on

4

the coach slept, as if they had all celebrated the night before and were catching up on their rest here.

The drunk was a big man, dressed in eastern clothes with a hard hat on his round, dark head. The hat canted to an angle as he slept, and when after a time he roused he made no effort to straighten it.

He fumbled diligently through a pocket and found a pint bottle better than half full, and worked out the cork. Then, turning, he saw her glance upon him and grinned. There was something in the grin that frightened her, a wolfish gloating in the prominent black eyes that made her flesh crawl.

"Hello, cutie." He extended the bottle. "I must have been snowed when I got on, not to see you. Have a drink."

She shook her head. "No . . . thank you."

"Ah, come on. Don't gimme airs. Goldfield ain't no place for airs, and you can have a worse friend than Dick Butler."

She turned her head away. He reached out, his heavy fingers clutched her shoulder and he pulled her around.

"You didn't hear me, I guess. Take a drink."

He shoved the bottle into her face. The next instant it slid from his hand and fell into her lap, spilling whiskey across her gray skirt. She gasped, straightening as the alcohol soaked through the cloth, wetting her skin, and drew away as her temper broke loose. But the man was no longer sitting at her side.

Gilbert Lorran had been following the action from beneath his half-closed eyes. He was not asleep and had no impulse to sleep. He would have interfered sooner, but the last thing he wanted to do was attract attention to himself. This, though, had gone too far. He reached out suddenly across the narrow space and grabbed Butler, his right hand seizing the coat collar, his left tightening about the drunk's throat. He jerked Butler off the seat, onto his knees on the swaying floor.

For an instant Butler was too surprised to move, then he clawed at the side coat pocket which held his gun. Lorran let go of the collar and knocked the hand away. His fingers tightened on the thick throat and he said in low warning,

"Behave yourself."

But Dick Butler had no idea of behaving. His whiskey-bathed mind swam in a red curtain as his hair-trigger temper flamed. He tried to hit Lorran in the side. The fingers on his throat tightened convulsively. He reached up, catching Lorran's thumb and bending it back, trying to break the grip, to snap the bone.

Lorran let go and used his left hand to club the side of Butler's neck, a blow he had seen used effectively in prison. He struck below the ear and watched the man fall forward into his lap, the head lolling. He heard the girl's sharp drawn breath and the excited sounds from the other passengers as they waked, and he paid no attention. He shoved the unconscious man away to fall prone in the little aisle and leaned out of the window, shouting to the driver above his head.

"Pull up. We've got some trouble down here."

There was a loud curse from the box, the coach lurched as the squealing brakes bit against the iron tires

6

and the driver hauled back on his six-horse team. Then he came down over the wheel like a long-legged spider.

Before he hit the ground Lorran had the door open and was outside, dragging the unconscious man after him as unceremoniously as a sack of wheat. He dumped him on the rock-strewn earth, turning him over with the toe of his boot as the driver joined him.

"He was drunk, annoying the lady."

The driver was a slack-faced man with a lantern jaw and deep set eyes that bulged now.

"Jeese, that's Dick Butler . . ."

"So . . . what about it?"

"He's a gambler, speculator, mining man and dangerous as hell. He killed two men in Austin couple of years back."

Lorran stooped, pulled the gun from Butler's pocket and hurled it into the brush.

"Come on. Let him sleep it off."

"I don't dare leave him; he'll raise Ned when he catches up with me."

"You don't dare not to," Lorran said. "Get back on that box. I'm in a hurry to get to Goldfield."

The driver straightened to protest angrily, but he swallowed the words as he lifted his face. Lorran's eyes were chip blue and hard as obsidian. The driver took a fast look at the rest of this unfamiliar passenger.

He saw a narrow, strong-boned face, the smooth-shaven cheeks somewhat hollow and heavily tanned, surprisingly young beneath the white hair not completely covered by the wide-brimmed, flat-crowned hat. The clothes were good, hickory pants stuffed into laced boots, a white shirt of good material, a long-tailed black broadcloth coat. There was nothing of the town about them. This could be a gambler, a mining operator, but someone who belonged to the outdoors, with the stillness of solitude like a wall around him.

The heavy revolver supported by the belt crystallized the driver's impression. He was afraid of Dick Butler and what Butler might do, but that was in the future. At the moment he was facing Lorran, and he had the intuition that if he refused to pull ahead he would join Butler on the ground, that this stranger was eminently capable of shooting him and driving the stage on into town himself.

Without a sound he climbed back to his seat. Lorran did not wait to see him reach it. He swung into the coach and took the seat beside the girl, pulling the door shut after him.

The men inside had been peering out, talking excitedly, but his re-entry was a signal for silence and now they watched him covertly from the corners of their eyes, sensing the latent violence in the lithe body.

The girl was fearful, not liking the idea of his changing seats, but as the coach began to move he said in a soft voice,

"I'm sorry about your dress. I should have interfered sooner, but it didn't occur to me he'd go so far."

She looked up uncertainly, and noted the way his carefully chiseled lips curved and the laugh wrinkles grew as he smiled. The smile changed the whole face, destroying the austerity, bringing it alive. Yet the eyes remained remote and glacial.

8

"It's all right," she said. "And thank you. I don't know what I'd have done . . . I heard what the driver said about that man. Will he make trouble for you?"

Lorran's shrug said that it was not important.

"What will happen to him, alone, away out here in the desert?"

"He'll have a sore neck when he comes around, and he'll catch a ride on one of the freight wagons."

"Will he try to find you, to get back at you? I'm sorry if you'll be in trouble because of me."

He made a small, wry grimace. He was in trouble; he had known trouble for a very long time, but it had nothing to do with this girl or his rough treatment of Dick Butler.

"Everyone's always in some kind of trouble, Miss . . ."

"Emma Bondford. Do you live in Goldfield?"

"I'm going to, for a while."

"Oh." Her disappointment was plain. "I hoped you could tell me something about it."

"Then you don't live there? I thought maybe your family was there."

"I haven't any family. My father . . . died . . . I have a position. I'm going to be governess for a widower's children . . . a man named Amos Frost."

"Oh?" He did not quite keep the startled lift out of his voice, but he did squeeze down the hot surge of emotion.

"You know him?"

"I'm not familiar in Goldfield." He evaded a direct answer, for he did not intend telling anyone that he had come a long way to find Amos Frost, the first of the four. His instinct was to cut off the conversation at once, but he checked himself. Anyone connected with Amos Frost in any way was of vital interest to him. He meant to study the man, to search out his weaknesses and through them force him to destroy himself. To do this he needed contact with Frost, and what better introduction could there be than through the governess?

It was unexpected luck, and he set himself to begin here, where there were other ears than hers listening, to create the new image, the new personality.

"I haven't seen the town yet, but I can tell you about what it's like, because all mining towns, boom towns are much the same. I hear there are already eight or nine thousand people. The story is that the mines are so rich they paid their own way from grassroots even though the ore has to be hauled ninety miles to Mills' railroad and shipped another two hundred to the smelter." His smile offered her sympathy. "You'll probably find it pretty lonely for awhile, I mean for other women to talk to. The kind you'll see won't be the kind you're used to."

She was already lonely, painfully alone and unsure, and she found it helpful, strengthening, to talk with someone other than the disinterested trainmen and stage employees. She reached out to try to keep the talk alive.

"Are you going into mining, Mr. — I don't believe I know your name."

"My apology. Mont Christian. Yes, I'll probably do a little mining; it's about the only business I know." He was pleased to see her interest, and spent the rest of the miles in telling her about other mining camps that he had known.

At last the coach rolled over the low hills and across the flat beside Columbia mountain, coming at a run, a final flourish, into the new town site. He helped her to the ground, then turned to give the driver a hand at unloading the baggage from the boot, concerned with his own four heavy boxes packed at the bottom.

As he finished he heard the girl call his name and went toward where she stood on the sidewalk with a short, heavily built, big-faced man.

"Mr. Christian," she said, "I want you to meet Mr. Frost." She looked at her employer. "Mr. Christian was very kind to me on the coach. A man named Butler was annoying me."

"Butler? Dick Butler? Yes, he would. I appreciate your help, Mr. Christian."

Frost thrust out a thick-palmed hand. Lorran took it deliberately, possessively, but shook it only briefly. He watched closely for some sign of recognition, but none came. Frost hardly glanced at him as he said,

"Welcome to Goldfield. It's the greatest town in the country, bar none. If I can help you, just let me know. I've got the assay office down the street, four doors below the new hotel. You can't miss it."

"I'll remember," Gil Lorran said. "I'm certain you'll be seeing me. We'll be doing some business together."

He watched them move away through the crowd that had gathered around the arriving stage, then went back to collect his luggage and the four heavy boxes, and with the help of a hack driver carried them to a third-floor room in the Goldfield Hotel.

He was not surprised that Frost had not recognized him. As far as he knew the assayer had only seen him twice, and that had been a long ten years before. His hair had been black then, his face round and boyish, unmarked by suffering.

He sat down on the soft, clean bed and looked around him at the elegance of the new building, the red carpet underfoot, the ornate brass bedstead, the glowing furniture. It was a far cry from the Snake Pit. But it was not the end of the road.

Much had been done already. The preparations had gone better than he had dared to hope for — never easy — but each small success mounting toward a formidable power.

Now he was here. Now the first quarry was in sight. Now it would begin, the retribution to be visited upon those four who had so nearly broken him. Slowly. So that each should know the agony of his own disintegration. They had begun it, and had laughed.

CHAPTER
TWO

Gilbert Lorran's birthright had been good health, and a good nature, outgiving and trustful of his fellow men. But the years of prison had played havoc with him. For seven years he had no more than existed, caught in a hopeless nightmare from which there appeared no surcease except death.

He would rather have died, but the instinct to survive is rooted in man's primate ancestors, and life clings even when suffering has driven the human animal into insanity.

Lorran had come very close to that point. His mind was reaching backward into dark oblivion that afternoon as he lay on the sharp gravel, his body pinioned within a minimum circle of mobility around the short heavy chain that fastened his ankle cuff to the ring bolt in the floor. He had not moved a muscle for hours, for days as far as he knew.

The Snake Pit in which he lay was an irregularly round cell burrowed into the bank of composite rock that formed one wall of the Territorial Prison. A narrow tunnel, ten yards long, isolated the pit deep within the ground and gave entrance to it from the stone-paved exercise yard, and was blocked at both ends by doors made of heavy iron straps bolted together in a four-inch-square grille pattern. The cell was roughly ten feet across, the ceiling not five feet high, too low to permit him to stand erect, but this was no longer of any importance to him. His struggles to move at all were behind him.

There was hardly more light in the hole during the day than at night, for the tunnel made a bend. Only at midday did the sun send a shaft down the vent hole, not as large around as his arm, that had been punched through the rock from the top of the bank fifteen feet above.

The darkness was the only comfort he had. In the yard and in the cell blocks above ground the temperature of the Arizona afternoon was a dry, shriveling weight above a hundred and twenty degrees. Lorran lay semiconscious, open mouthed, gasping the air that felt like molten lava into his straining lungs. Under the coarse cloth of the prison suit his body was greased with thick sweat. His straggling beard, his face and hands were crusted with grit, for he had been rubbing his head into the filthy ground in his torment.

In seven years this was his first time in the Pit, and it was living up to its grisly reputation. He had heard about it from the first, for it held a horrible, hypnotic fascination for all of the prisoners. There were stories of men going wildly mad in the lonely dark heat, of their freezing to death with neither solid door not blanket to protect them from winter's bitter blasts. There was the fear of scorpions that crept through the open grilles, crawled against your flesh for warmth and stung with a thousand poison legs when your movement startled them. There was helpless terror of sadistic guards who were said to throw a deadly sidewinder in with a captive who had incurred their anger.

He did not know if he had such companions. He had lost track of time and did not know that he had been chained there for a week. He was alone and beyond feeling anything except the constant itch of biting sand fleas to which he was host and the sharp pain that accompanied any movement, where the rusty leg iron chafed the broken and festered skin of his ankle.

He lay alternately silent and unconsciously moaning, no longer aware that once a day a cup of water and a chunk of bread were placed within his reach.

When he heard the rasp of the iron hinges now it meant nothing. He did not even open his eyes. Not until he felt the brutal cuff unlocked and dropped from his leg did he rouse, and then only vaguely, not guessing that this signaled the end of his ordeal here. But the guard's boot prodded into his side and the expressionless voice ordered him;

"Go on, crawl on out, if you can."

He lifted painfully to his hands and knees and obediently crawled, the loose pebbles of the dished floor digging into his palms and scraping the skin from his knees.

The grille at the end of the tunnel stood open and he crawled through into the exercise yard, struck by the blistering sun and blinded by the intense light so that an involuntary cry of pain escaped him. On the guard's urging he used the gate's bars as a hand ladder to drag himself upright, and stood swaying perilously on his weakened legs.

The guard yanked the gate from his grasp and slammed it closed, leaving Lorran without support, poking the barrel of his rifle into the unsteady back, careless that the prisoner all but collapsed.

"Back to the cell block with you. Maybe you'll think twice the next time you feel like escaping."

He took a stumbling, ragged course down the yard toward the block of concrete cages. The escape try had not been planned, but a spontaneous act of desperation that, had he stopped to think of, he would not have made. In all of his years there only three men had made the attempt, and two of them had failed almost at the start. The third stayed free for three days, and then he was returned by the Mojave Apaches who lived along the river. They collected the standing reward of a hundred dollars for a returned prisoner, and the man was beaten so thoroughly that he died.

In the hope of the moment Lorran had forgotten this. The only way of escape was through death, and one prisoner had chosen to take this route, and hanged himself. Lorran was among those assigned to the burial detail. In the summer most burials were performed in the evening, after sundown, when the terrific heat was slightly lessened.

The graveyard was outside the prison wall on top of the small plateau above the river junction, for the Gila wound down out of the northeast and joined the Colorado here, in flood times creating a lake a mile wide, swift, turbulent, treacherous. The ground of the plateau was the same composite pebble and sand, cemented by the ages, as the bank out of which the cells had been hacked, and digging the shallow grave had been slow and hard, so that it was well after dark before the task was finished and the guards had ordered the return into the prison.

Brashly, Lorran had dropped flat behind one of the boards used as headboards and laid quietly, listening to the scuff of feet as the detail marched in lock-step through the gate. He knew that he would soon be missed, but he rose and ran mindlessly, and in his panic he fell into the slough that made a wide swath between the high ground and the river. The splash was heard, the dogs were released and ran him down. He was dragged back up the hill, whipped at the post in the middle of the yard and cast into the Snake Pit. Reaction to that snuffing of that small, quick flame of hope had been a crushing total surrender. Whatever would come next he did not care.

He reached the cell block, a flat, sheared-off face of the mountain into which was set a row of double strap-iron doors leaving the caves behind them open to the weather. The rooms were all identical, only distinguished by metal numerals above the doors. Carved out of the rock, nine feet long and eight wide, each was lined by a tier of bunks on either side, three beds in each tier, an eighteen-inch-wide shelf for each man. There was no furniture, not so much as a bowl in which to wash, yet six men were confined behind each grille through the years, surviving the summer's oven heat and winter's blasts, or not surviving.

Lorran's guard unlocked the outer door, shoved the unprotesting prisoner through into the narrow safety gap, unlocked the inner door and with a heavy push sent Lorran reeling, falling to the rock floor between the bunks.

He was dimly aware that the cell was empty, the men not yet returned from the day's work detail of repairing crumbling sections of the walls. Laboriously he climbed to the center bunk in the left hand tier, his bunk, for he would be mauled by his roommates if he were caught lying in another's. This was their single symbol of individuality, the nearest thing they could claim as a possession, and bunk rights were jealously maintained.

He stretched flat, on his back, not caring whether the men ever returned, except Travis. He could talk with Travis. In the rest of them he had no interest, although for more than six years he had lived in this close physical proximity with them. They were a segment of the famous "lifers" of the Territorial Prison at Yuma — the Hell Hole, the most dreaded prison of the West — killers, animal-like, humorless and further brutalized by the degradation of this pitiless incarceration. They boasted of their senseless murders, their robberies and rapes and took sadistic pleasure in human suffering.

He had had to fight for his place among them, to beat Dave Porter senseless to prove his equality to the bully, but he was accepted, because he too was serving a life sentence from which there was no appeal, no hope of pardon.

Long ago he had left off claiming innocence. No one cared. No one listened. No one believed. No one had believed him at his trial, and it had come not to matter even to himself. There was no privacy, so that even to Travis he had never told his story.

The grating of the gates, the disturbance of the returning group waked him, from sleep or torpor he did not know. He rolled onto his elbow and watched them shuffle in, and felt a dull disappointment that his only friend was not among them.

"Where's Travis?"

No one commented on his release from the Snake Pit; there was no longer curiosity in any of them. Dave Porter grinned at him, malice in his wicked chalk-blue eyes and in the pale, inside-out lips that gaped like a wound within his coarse beard. Dave had been convicted of burning a settler's cabin with three small children inside, and had escaped hanging only because the chief witness had fumbled the identification and because of Porter's reputation as an Indian-killer.

"Lucky bastard's got consumption. They dumped him in Isolation."

"Consumption." It was the name of doom here. A third of the inmates died of the disease, weakened as they were by bad food and the conditions under which they labored, and neither the guards nor the warden were immune. Five guards had succumbed in Lorran's time. The news shocked him as nothing had in many years. Travis was his only tie to human dignity. Travis had never bragged about his misdeeds. Travis had befriended him at the kangaroo court to which all new arrivals were subjected. Big Pedro, a huge Mexican brute feared by all the prisoners, had hung Lorran up by his thumbs for amusement's sake and Travis had cut him free, then backed Pedro into a coward's retreat and destroyed his overrule. Now Travis was stricken.

"How bad is he?"

Porter chuckled. "He'll die. They'll put him in a sack and plant him like a piece of spoiled meat, and his troubles will be over."

There had been no shroud of any kind around the man Lorran had helped to bury, and he said so.

"For a common stiff, no," Porter laughed again. "But the warden and the doctor and the guards are so scared of catching the fever themselves that they make one of us wrap up that kind of a body before we take it out of the sick cell, to keep it from contaminating anything."

Memory stirred in Lorran, and an association that sent a quivering coldness through him. He lay back, closing his eyes, and his mind began to come alive, to push back the oppressive numbness. It touched tentatively on the memory, drew away and returned more boldly. He did not hear the desultory talk around him, hypnotized by his evolving thoughts, and by the time the guard arrived to conduct them across to the mess hall for the evening meal he was ready to look squarely at the dangerous idea.

They marched in lockstep, Lorran at the end of the line. The way passed the high bluff into which the Snake Pit was dug and the Isolation cell beyond that. Lorran looked intently at the grille but could not see inside, because the floor of that cubicle was at an elevated level, reached by an upward slanting ramp.

His mind held focused on that door as he ate the unsavory, watery gravy poured over the mound of corn mush, as he was released afterward with the others for a free period in the yard. When the line broke apart he moved without apparent aim back toward the cell door, wary of the guards posted on the wall above and the two who patroled the yard. Close to the door he turned his back on it, watching for a moment when no one was near, then twisted his head and called in a quiet but carrying voice.

"Travis, Travis, can you hear me?"

A sliding sound and the rattle of pebbles answered him, and then a dim movement beyond the double doors told him that his friend was at the bottom of the ramp. He shifted to face parallel to the bank and risked another look inside, in time to see Travis use the back of his hand to wipe a dark smear from his lips.

"I just got out of the Pit. How is it with you?"

"Not good, kid, but you'd better keep away from here. If they catch you this close they'll think you're exposed and toss you in with me."

"Anyone in there to help you?"

There was a period of heavy coughing that started as grim laughter.

"The closest anybody comes is when they shove a dish under the door . . . Move on, here comes Herbert . . ." Travis swung and scrambled back up the ramp, and Lorran eased away, barely escaping the guard's attention.

CHAPTER
THREE

The brief contact whetted his appetite for the nebulous idea and brought it out of the realm of passing fancy, gave it a body that might be realized. It had been made a believable achievement in fiction. With careful planning it might be turned into reality for him. If he failed, death would reward his effort, but after the week in the Snake Pit death was preferable to the years of sub-life that was the only future before him.

Silently Lorran set about laying the groundwork for the wild plan triggered by Dave Porter's careless word. It would take patience; yet he could not delay. Travis might not live out the week, or he might be joined by another victim from another cell, a man who might give warning in the hope of currying favor with the guards.

His first decision must be a choice of ways to get himself transferred into the Isolation cell. The simplest was to attach himself to its entrance until terror of the contagion caused him to be confined there. But this would appear irrational, perhaps would invite suspicion. The longer way but the safer was to fake having the illness, for after the Snake Pit ordeal he was a logical candidate. There would only be this single chance in the foreseeable future, and he must not waste it, even at the risk that time might run out and trap him. And so he began.

At the morning roll call he answered his name with a paroxysm of coughing and was encouraged to find that every eye turned on him, the chronically nervous guards, the ranks of prisoners and particularly his own cell mates. It was not difficult to be convincing. He had only to think of the agony of the Pit.

He repeated the performance that evening at the free period in the yard, again before the full audience, and this time he bit the inside of his mouth until it bled. The self-inflicted pain and the heavy demand on his lungs left him weak and shaking, men moved away from him, and his hope hardened. But it was a long week before he was ushered at the end of a gun barrel to face the warden in the open air outside the man's office.

The warden made no effort to hide his fear of the plague. The doctor was innured to sympathy by years of practice on the frontier, and his examination was cavalier.

"Yes, that's consumption," he said.

Lorran was marched back to his cell and ordered to pick up the thin tick on which he slept. He ignored the men he was leaving, who pulled away from him as far as possible and cursed him for having brought sickness among them. Then, dragging his steps, struggling to hide the elation that coursed through him, he walked to the Isolation cell, heard the gates bolted behind him, and crawled up the slanting passage.

In relief he saw that the room held no one except Lem Travis, who lay huddled against the far wall, his wasted body uncovered, not moving to see the new arrival.

The voice was a tired whisper. "Who is it?"

"Gil Lorran."

The spider-thin arms and legs thrashed around and Travis sat up, his watery eyes staring. "Gil . . . kid . . . Oh God damn."

Lorran did not explain. After the years of keeping his own counsel, with every man suspicious of the other and ready to betray his companions for the profit of a trifling favor, he would not risk his plan by confiding even in Travis. He had succeeded this far, and now would come the waiting.

It lasted four weeks, and physically they were the least onerous weeks he had spent in the prison. There was no work detail, no schedule, and the food thrust under the door morning and evening was somewhat better than that slopped to them in the dining hall. Travis told him with bitter humor that they were being fattened up to die. The slanting tunnel and a larger air shaft drew a fresh current through the room and kept the underground temperature at a more bearable level than in his old cell.

Travis was resigned to death, even looking forward to it for release, and Lorran, though he would not have chosen to lose his friend this way, found it hard to curb his impatience. The slender thread of life spinning toward its inevitable end held only misery for the dying one, and the slow passage of time was a cruel mockery to Lorran.

The waiting. The waiting. It built pressure in spite of all the control he could command. Over and over he rehearsed in his mind the things that he must do when the time was finally come. There were no promises of success; there was only the opportunity, to live, free beyond the wall or to die in the attempt.

He tried to quiet the mounting tension by talking, and Travis seemed to draw something from recollection, from trading stories. For the first time in seven years Lorran talked about the four men and what they had done to him and about his life before prison.

His father had been in California in 49', in Virginia City for the silver strike in 61'. Lorran was born there and when that camp died the two of them had wandered over the West, prospecting, until his father's death in a mine accident. In Tombstone he had found a promising reef, had taken samples to an assayer whom he thought could be trusted, a man named Amos Frost. Frost had reported the samples worthless, but three men had immediately appeared and tried to buy the claim.

"I wouldn't sell. I thought I could make a mine," Lorran said. "I took samples to another assayer, and when I went to his office to get the report I found him dead, murdered. That's when I made my second mistake. I didn't think much of the law there. I didn't want to get mixed up in a killing, so I just left. But several people saw me, and the next day I was arrested. They held me in jail for trial, but Frost and the men he had sent to buy my claim stirred up a mob. They broke me out and already had a rope around my neck and were hanging me when the sheriff stopped them and cut me down."

He opened the neck of his striped prison shirt and pulled it away, showing the old rope scar that still remained. "I got this for a souvenir, and a life sentence from the judge, and Frost got my mine."

Travis' eyes were closed, but he had listened with genuine interest. "How do you know he got it?"

"I had a letter from a newspaper man, two years after I came here. Frost and his three friends filed on it as soon as my claim lapsed. They took over a million dollars out of that ground."

Travis lay silent for a long while. There seemed nothing to say to what Lorran had told him. Then he commented sardonically, "I believe you, kid. Most of the men here yell that they're innocent to begin with, but then they start bragging about all they've done. They belong locked up."

Lorran had never questioned, nor ever decided in his mind about his friend. Now he said, "You were innocent?"

Travis moved on his pallet and an anger that had seemed long dead flushed his face. "I was guilty, all right I killed my best friend. He stole my wife."

"Want to talk about it?"

The sick man shrugged. "Why not? I was mining in Mexico, and I asked him to look out for her while I was south of the border. When I got home I found out he'd lied to her, told her I'd been killed. They'd been married over a year. I went out of my head and shot him. She died about six months later and I'll be dead pretty quick. None of it seems very important now . . . How old are you, kid?"

"Twenty-nine."

"Hell. I'm sorry you got sick. I must have given it to you in the cell." He rolled his head away in self-accusation.

Before he thought, Lorran had said, "But I'm not sick."

Travis rolled back quickly, his eyes clouding with suspicion. He waited for Lorran to speak again and when he did not said in a flat voice, "What the hell's going on, then?"

Lorran cursed himself silently. His first impulse was to lie, to claim that the guard had caught him loitering outside the cell, but lying went against his grain. He gave the man a twisted smile.

"I guess I owe it to you to tell you. I faked a cough and bleeding to get in here. I mean to use you, Travis."

The sick man looked at him, bewildered. "I'd appreciate knowing how, and for what."

Lorran moved across the cell and sat cross-legged at the man's head, beginning to speak softly, watching his friend's face for the reaction. Unwanted, the thought came to him that if Travis gave any sign of raising a cry he could be quickly quieted, and with it came the shock of knowledge of what the prison had done to him. For he knew that he would kill Travis rather than surrender this chance.

27

He said, "Dave Porter told me that when a consumptive dies they make another prisoner put the body in a sack, in here, before they take it outside and bury it. It made me remember something from a long time ago. When I had a mother she used to read to me. She read me a book called the *Count of Monte Cristo*. You ever read it?"

Travis' eyes showed an impatience, as if he thought Lorran was trying to lead away from the question that now hung between them.

"I never read much of anything. What's that got to do with . . . ?"

Lorran nodded. "That's the key. Listen to me. It was a story about a man in prison like me, for something he didn't do, and another prisoner who died. They put the body in a sack and went away. The live man took the sack off the body and got into it himself, and they threw him into the ocean. He escaped that way."

Comprehension grew slowly in Travis' eyes. Lorran felt the tension coil tight within him. This was the moment. Automatically his hands shaped themselves, ready to reach for the shrunken throat, to stifle any sound that might start there. For a long while Travis lay motionless, without expression, as Lorran watched all of the implications reach him, sort themselves out and form a pattern, as he waited, poised, not breathing.

Then Travis' mouth spread slowly in a weak grin, his eyes gained a bright speculation.

"You've got guts, kid." The voice was an awed whisper. "Do you really think it would work?"

Lorran relaxed a degree of his tension. "It worked in the book."

"They haven't got an ocean here. They put you in a hole and cover you with dirt."

"I think I've got that figured out."

Travis tried to laugh but broke into coughing, and then lay gasping, spacing his words between his deep breaths.

"I'm glad you told me. I hope you make it. I'll feel better about going out. Like I'm doing something good. Like to help you."

A wave of guilt swept over Lorran and left him weak. He reached for the other's chill hand. "Lem, did you know, I was ready to choke you if you objected."

"I don't blame you. This place kind of peels a man down to basics." He squirmed onto his side and raised onto his elbow. "What happened to your Count after he got away?"

"The kind of thing that can happen in a book. A prisoner had bragged about knowing where a treasure was buried. The Count found it. It made him one of the richest men in the world . . ."

Travis interrupted him, rolling onto his back and breaking into sudden cawing laughter that again changed to a paroxysm of coughs, drawing his knees up against his chest to fight it. Blood rose in his mouth and he spat it out, then lay exhausted, weakly patting Lorran's knee.

"What's so funny?" Lorran asked.

"Later . . . gotta rest . . . tell you something . . ."

Travis closed his eyes and immediately sunk into a stupor, and Lorran wondered if this might not be the approach of death. But the afternoon wore on, and the shallow breathing continued, grew less ragged. The guard shoved the evening plates in under the door and Lorran scrambled down to bring them up. In the dimness of the fading day he saw that Travis' eyes were open, a mysterious eagerness in them, but he did not speak until both had eaten, then he gestured Lorran to his side.

"I've got a surprise for you, kid. A present. Four hundred pounds of gold."

Lorran felt a prickling at the back of his neck. Travis' mind was going. He put a hand on his friend's shoulder, pressing it. "Take it easy, Lem. Easy."

Travis grinned. "I'm not nuts. It's true. That's what was so funny. Just like your Count. It's down in Mexico, in the Sierra Madre del Norte. Do you know that country?"

"A little." Still Lorran thought it was the product of a fevered imagination, a hallucination sparked by the Monte Cristo tale, but if Travis wanted to talk, he would listen. "My father and I prospected it when I was a boy. The Yaquis drove us out."

Travis nodded. "I know. Lots of them in there, lots of Commanches and Apaches, raiding down across the border, and a lot of white toughs too, out for a little scalp hunting. When I was in there it was about as remote from Mexico City's authority as it was from London, and the whole political situation was in chaos. But there's a hacienda, an old one, been in the same

30

family for three-hundred years, the Llano Colorado. You know it?"

"No."

"Well, we were working a mine about twenty-five miles away from it. That whole country is highly mineralized. This one day I was out scouting for a lost mine that was supposed to be around there somewhere. I heard some shots, a long way off but in the direction of our camp. I headed that way, being careful. When I got there my two partners were dead and our sacks of hi-grade were gone. From the tracks it looked like there'd been three Americans."

"They left a trail a mile wide, figuring there wasn't anybody to follow them. They took our mules and headed for the Cerro de Chivato. Do you remember that country? There's nothing worse in North America, only a few trails through the hills, left by the Spaniards and their slave Indians. If you get off of them you're lost, you'll never get out."

He paused, taking deliberate, spaced breaths, and then went on. "I caught them camped in a draw that leads up over the mountain. I waited for night and then slipped in and cut their throats, but one woke up and we had a fight. The mules and horses stampeded and I got a bullet in my shoulder. I knew I couldn't take the gold out in that shape, on foot, so I hid it in a sort of cave, not a deep one, threw the bodies in on top of it and covered them with rocks. As a rule Indians won't disturb the dead, and I figured the bones would mark the place for me when I came back."

He shook his head slowly, in resignation. "I never got back. I barely made the hacienda. My shoulder was infected and I was out of my head with fever. The family was away, the Anayas, but the major domo took me in and nursed me. He and the peons were Opatas, Indians who had lived on that land for generations. Then they put me in a mule train headed for Hermosillo, and there I joined an American party going to Tucson."

"I was still sick and weak when I got home and found what I told you about, and killed him, and landed here. That's twenty years ago. This is the first time I've talked about it. It ought to be still there."

Lost mines, hidden treasures, fortunes with curses upon them, dazzling, tempting Loreleis that haunted the barren mountains and deserts and drew men on like mirages in the sand — Lorran had heard their songs sung all of his life. He hid his smile. But he would let Travis spin out his dream skein. It was the only way he could repay him for the favor he would extract.

"Thank you," he said solemnly. "How do I find the spot?"

Travis was too weak to notice the small doubt in the voice. "Go to the hacienda. Somebody there will remember me. They'll show you the trail to the mine. It's called the Santa Barbara. The trace up the mountain is easy to find, up a draw with a rock that looks like a horse's head at the mouth. The entrance is narrow, runs between high chalk walls, but about a mile up it widens into a little park with a seep spring. The cave is on the west side. The pile of rocks is plain, not like the rest of the hillside. You'll find the bones and underneath them about fifty thousand dollars worth of practically pure gold. Now tell me what your Count did with his money."

"He ran down his enemies and made them destroy themselves."

Travis grimaced. "Then he wasn't any better than they were, was he? You take that gold and forget about Frost; go somewhere and start fresh. Take a good look at a man who let hatred ruin him. Look what it got me."

"All right," said Lorran. "I'll go to Europe and be a king." What did it matter what he said, since there was no gold, since if he won free he would be broke, an escaped convicted murderer who must spend the rest of his life like any other fugitive?

Travis looked at him thoughtfully, and this time read his mind. "No," he said. "No you won't. You don't believe me, although I've told you the truth. You won't go for the gold. And if you do, you've been in here too long. You'll be sick with vengeance, no more curable than I am." His eyes changed, widened. "Maybe you'll have caught the plague from being with me all this time. But it won't make difference in the end, one way or the other. I'm sorry for you, Lorran. I'm glad I won't be around to watch."

CHAPTER
FOUR

There were three more days while Travis sunk lower, laid unmoving and seldom spoke, and then at four-thirty in the afternoon he died, coughing and spilling out a final hemorrhage. Lorran had gone to him and held his head, kneeling behind him and supporting him until the body slumped forward and then flung backward in a reflex straightening.

The weeks had been long, and now they were over. Lorran was alone. He felt it sharply, with a touch of panic. While Travis had been there to talk to, the moment when he must act was pushed away, he need not face the actual, physical commitment to a course that had so slender a chance of succeeding. Now the odds against it loomed, and the consequences, if he were caught.

It would not work. No one escaped from Yuma. The guards would sense that the body in the sack was alive, they would drag him out and pitch him back into the Snake Pit, and there he would die.

He shook himself. He retreated to his mattress and sat, slapping his head with his palms, gulping in air. He forced his mind to remember the rehearsed details of the plan. He shut away all other thought.

First, there must be more waiting. There must be darkness. He lay down, commanding his body to relax, member by member. He counted, to a thousand and then again, slowly, by the monotony of the numbers enduring the dragging hours.

He waited until the guard brought the plates, went down for them, but could not eat He listened to the dull sounds of the exercise period, to the echo of the gates being closed on the prisoners down the line. Then, with barely light to see, he went to the grille and shouted.

A guard came, stopping well back from the door. "What are you yelling about?"

Lorran gripped the bars. "Travis just died."

"Good riddance."

A burst of rage made him shake the iron bands like an ape in a cage, but he bit his mouth until his head cooled down to where he could think. He waited where he was while the guard went away and returned, dragging a sack of heavy brown canvas, and ordered him to put Travis' body into it and "Throw it down here by the gate." Again the guard left, to gather a burial detail. Lorran stepped into the sack, lay down against the grille and pulled the drawstring tight, holding onto it inside.

When he heard the shuffle of feet he stiffened himself as rigid as possible, keeping his breathing to slow, shallow draughts. Then they had him, lifting him roughly, carrying him out of the yard. He had a vision of the passage, past the square tower where the Gatling gun was constantly trained on the exercise area, under the arched tunnel in the thick wall, a right turn, and a short walk to the graveyard, and there he was dumped while his grave was dug.

They had only the afterglow of the day to work in, and they hurried, anxious to be rid of their dangerous burden. He was lifted again and dropped into the fresh depression, and a new panic touched him as earth was shoveled heavily upon him.

He fought for control, staying quiet until he felt the weight of earth rise over his chest and head, until sounds were blotted out, until the jar of falling clods told him that the work was finished. Then, straining not to give away to the panic, he eased one arm from the sack and burrowed with it toward the surface. One last rock fell on his fingers, bringing pain and further fright. They were still there. Again he began to count, waiting until the numbers told him that they must surely be gone, then he began an earnest labor, pawing the dirt away from his hand, feeling the freedom of movement spread to his wrist, to his forearm. With his other hand beneath him he worked his body upward, following his upthrust arm, inching worm-like through the loose soil.

By now he expected sudden discovery, but he could wait no longer. Pushing through the gravel with his head he was startled when it suddenly broke free, when the night air wrapped coolly around his sweating face, and he drew in a ragged breath.

It was totally dark. The detail was gone. A thousand yards away the lights of the prison glowed and the voices of the patrolling guards came hollowly over the wall.

He worked faster now, clawing, wriggling, and finally slid from his cocoon and pulled his feet free. He lay across the piled rocks for a moment, shaking, and then began a slither to the edge of the knoll, over that, and down the slope into darkness.

Below him lay the wide river, from this height looking like a lazy snake, oily, sinuous in the starlight. Like a snake himself, on his belly, he headed toward it. He reached the slough and crept through that, bouyed in spots by the few inches of water. Then the water was deeper, the tule reeds thinned, and at last he felt the swift sucking of the main current of the open river.

There was no time yet to think of being free. His direction was already chosen and it was still fraught with hazard. He could not go upstream, the current was too strong, and he could not go across country, the dogs would out race him. The river swept toward the border, thirty miles away, and along its banks the Indians had watchful eyes. Yet that was the least of the possible risks.

He slid into the water and found a soft footing, wading out to waist depth. The surface rushed past him silent, shimmering with the broken reflection of stars. Across its width floated dark spots of jetsum, branches, shrubs, a board brought down from many miles above.

And then he saw what he was seeking, a broken tree trunk moving slowly in the center of the river, well upstream. He began to swim, downstream, angling out to intercept its course. It came faster than he had guessed, swept past him, and he called on all of the reserve strength he had to chase it. He would have missed it but that it hung up for a moment on a jutting jam of brush.

He touched it, grabbed at it, and hauled himself up to lie along its length. There, on its safety, with his arms snugged around a branch stub, he sagged down. Emotions hammered at him, the trauma of the years, of the last month, this night, Travis' death, and the terrifying experience of being buried alive. He began to quake. And then he wept. He was free. Not yet safely away, but free.

He thought that he stayed awake and watched, but the lights of a river steamer passing close startled him. He looked upward, expecting to be detected, but the boat veered away from the obstacle and went on. When he waked again it was mid afternoon, and he had no idea how far he had floated.

The tree had swirled in and lodged against the north bank of the river, on a sandy bar. In the black and white striped prison suit he would be easily seen, if he had not been already. He stripped it off, snagged it on a branch below the water line, and lay down in the shallows, soaking away the grime on his body. It was safer, he thought, to lie there, listening for sound among the deep tules, ready to push his tree into the current again and swim beneath it should he hear a warning rustle, than to continue on in daylight.

Nothing disturbed him until sundown and then a voice carried to him across the water. He lifted his head carefully and saw a canoe headed up the river, paddled by a white man and an Indian. The white man pointed to the sand bar and they swung the canoe toward it.

There was no place that Lorran could retreat nor any better hiding place than he had. He could only lie there and wait.

But apparently the canoe was not searching for him. It landed on the far side of the bar and the two men, unconcerned, set about making a camp for the night. They were perhaps an eighth of a mile away and through the branches he watched them unload gear, a rifle, blankets. They built a fire and cooked a meal and then sat smoking as the darkness gathered.

Lorran waited, gathering himself, thinking ahead. When the night was an hour old the men rolled themselves in the blankets, their feet against the dying fire, and slept. Lorran waited another while, until he judged that they had fallen into the first deep slumber, then left his tree and naked stalked cautiously toward them.

The stars cast an eerie luminescence across the land and the oily water. A coyote yammered somewhere on the higher ground. Lorran approached the Indian silently, and the blow he struck just behind the man's ear was carefully timed. The sleeper grunted once and tried to roll and Lorran hit him again. This time he did not move, but the sound disturbed the white man. He struggled to sit up, flinging back the blanket, reaching for the short gun at his side. Lorran leaped, kicking the gun away, landed on top of the man and they sprawled together.

Without clothes, wet from the river, Lorran made a form too slippery to hold, and though the white man fought, it was not for long. Again Lorran used the edge of his palm against the neck and felt the man go slack.

He rolled the man over, stripped him of his shirt and trousers and put them on and then saw the money belt around the thick waist. He unfastened it, found that it held fifty silver dollars, a twist of Mexican tobacco and a blackened pipe. The pipe and tobacco he left on the ground. He gathered the short gun and the rifle, a long-bladed knife from the Indian, a blanket, threw them and a part of the food into the canoe, and shoved the craft into the river. It was unwieldy, a hollowed log, but going downstream he could handle it.

The men he left on the bar would be all right. They would have sore heads when they waked, but they could walk a little way inland and soon find help from the Indians growing beans along the rich strip of soil beside the river.

Lorran gave them no further thought. They would survive, and he was free.

Free to do what? He had not thought past the almost insurmountable problem of escaping, that had been enough to occupy him. But now through the night he pondered. He was going into Mexico perforce. The story of Travis' gold recurred to him. It was probably a wild-goose chase, but what better way had he to spend the time while he mended himself from the prison warping?

He looked toward the heavens and smiled. "All right, Lem," he said aloud. "Let's just go have a look."

CHAPTER
FIVE

In the Sierra del Norte the Yaqui had never been conquered. They survived with their pride all the power that the Spanish and Mexicans threw against them for three hundred years. They had accommodated themselves to a few white settlers and made good ranch hands when they were well treated, but they were never enslaved like the other Indians of the region, and many still remembered their childhood training. Kill the *yori*, the whites who had stolen their land. Like their cousins, the Apaches, they still fought jealously for this land, sterile, barren, unwelcoming as it was.

It was into their mountains that Gilbert Lorran gradually made his way. Six months out of Yuma, his beard gone, his lined face smooth shaven, his white hair trimmed and combed, fresh clothes that fit covering the body that was losing its starved boniness, he looked little different from the mining men and scalp hunters who drifted through the area.

No one questioned these lean, hard men who filtered down across the border. Some were employed by mining companies looking for new mineral deposits, some searching for the fabled lost mines which legend said the Jesuits had hidden when they were driven out, some were keeping away from the lawmen of the States.

But withall the land was vast and empty. Years of intermittent revolutions, of Apache and Comanche raids made under the September moon had wiped out ranchito and village and left the once heavily-traveled Camino Real, the Silver Road, a mere trace through the uncaring hills.

Gilbert Lorran felt the ghostliness, and the belief that Travis' gold existed only in the sick man's fever dream increased. But it was a temporary goal to aim at, a way of working back into the world of the living. It was a time between, a period when he only wanted to float, with the freedom of choice, and he would not be disappointed to find that the trail he followed led to nothing.

But the hacienda Llano Colorado was there. Lorran rode into it leading a second mule but breaking the custom of the country in not hiring a mozo to run behind him, to care for the animals and gear. He dismounted in the dusty little square before the tiny whitewashed church and was made welcome by Juan Anaya, who was glad of any visitor to break the monotony of the days.

Anaya, a stocky man of forty with gray hair and gray Castilian eyes, took him into the dim adobe hall and talked at length of the family, who had lived here since the middle fifteen hundreds. When Lorran casually mentioned that his friend, Lem Travis, had had an accident in these parts, Anaya at once remembered.

A odd, prickling stirring of excitement seeped into Lorran. He asked about the mine, and yes, Anaya knew it, and he would send a guide with his guest in the morning.

At daybreak Anaya met him in the yard, assigned an Opata whom he said had been raised at the hacienda to show the way, and delicately suggested that the guest could be more pleasantly remembered if he had a name.

Gilbert Lorran had used half-a-dozen names in as many months, but now on impulse he smiled.

"Mont Christian," he said. He shook Anaya's hand and rode away.

It was a rough trail winding through low foothills, skirting a gorge that dropped abruptly from the shelf, which in places was so narrow that it would be impossible to turn a mule. Far to the east, like a green wall, rose the timbered slopes of the Tarahumares country, shutting the northwest corner off from the rest of Mexico with a barrier that few white men had crossed.

The mozo trotted ahead tirelessly, his bare feet impervious to the rocks of the worn path, and at dusk led them into a sheltered bowl, a surprising oasis. There was plenty of water, and Lorran was astonished to find quinces growing there, peaches, oranges, pomegranates, and the first bananas he had seen in Sonora, trees planted by the Spaniard so long ago that people could not remember. And there were the remains of two arastras, stonepaved grinding platforms where the early miners had ground their ore, with huge trees growing through the cracked slabs.

The mozo stood pointing toward a more modern smelting facility, set beside the creek; yet it too showed signs of being long deserted.

This then was the ancient mine that Travis had said he and his partners had located and worked. So far he had told the truth, but still Lorran was skeptical of the rest of the story. It was too wild a possibility to put credence in, to risk building hope on, because if he did and was then disappointed, it would be a double blow. Fifty thousand dollars was a staggering sum to simply pick off of the ground.

He schooled himself to be concerned only with what he saw. He walked to the mine shaft and peered down, seeing water six feet below, guessing that the old workings had flooded. A climbing ladder, a single pole notched on both sides for steps, disappeared down into the shaft, but he had no desire to test its strength. He turned back to the fire the mozo had built and asked if the man had been here before.

The Indian bobbed his head but cast a sharp glance around as if he feared they would be overheard, although they had seen no one since leaving the hacienda. Lorran returned to studying the place. There were no marks on the ground to indicate the presence of domestic animals, but there were many prints of deer, and he had seen turkeys, Mearns quail, and band-tailed pigeons on the ride in. With the fruit and the abundance of game, with water, this seemed an ideal valley, where a man could live out his life in peace.

44

Yet there was no sign that anyone had been here in many years. Since Travis' hasty departure?

He asked the mozo why such a place should be abandoned. The Indian rolled his eyes uncomfortably and said in a low voice, almost a whisper,

"Now it belongs to the ancient ones. They have taken it back."

He would say nothing more, and when Lorran waked in the morning he was gone.

Neither superstition nor being alone bothered Lorran. He shot a careless quail for breakfast, roasted it, filled his canteen and the water cask on the lead mule, then took his sight on the Cerro de Chivato and began the eastward climb.

The track he followed had been made by man but was almost obliterated by disuse. It led through a number of defiles as narrow as yesterday's trace, but here the walls of the little canyon rose above him so close that he could touch both sides at once. It turned up through a larger canyon, along a rising shelf where holes had been worn into the path by generations of pack animals. He guessed now that this was a section of the treasure road over which had been hauled the flood of gold and silver for the coffers of the king of Spain.

Lorran had a sensation of riding into the past. If Travis' imagination had run riot here, his too was rising, and he would not have been surprised to round a corner and come face to face with a Conquistador in helmet and breastplate, guarding a train of loaded burros.

But he saw no one, saw nothing out of the ordinary until ahead of him there rose the rock in the horsehead shape. Beneath it lay the entrance to the last draw. Again Travis' words were true.

It was hard now to remain above expectancy. He urged the mules and came to the park, exactly as Travis had described it. He looked along the west wall, holding his breath, and there saw the pile of stones, strewn now by animals, and white bones scattered among them.

He climbed down, working as if he were in a dream, his hands shaking as turmoil took hold of him. Casting the rocks and bones aside in careless haste he burrowed into the cave, and then stopped still, staring at the brown surface of a leather bag.

The gold was there. All of it. Travis' gift to him. Gilbert Lorran hauled it out, found the bags still sturdy, preserved by the dry mountain air, and tied them beneath the blankets on the mules.

As he worked, the many possibilities of what this fortune could mean to him grew like clouds of mist, rolling, changing shape in his mind, inexorably forming a rationale that filled his head to bursting, blotting out all argument that he might have made.

He had always been a loner, preferring solitude, originally wandering the wastelands with his father and then without him. In Tombstone he had only begun to find pleasure in the society of others when Frost had frauded him. In prison his only refuge had been in personal retreat. He had had Travis, yes, but now Travis was gone. There was no one with whom he could talk, no one who might reason against and dispel the sickness that took possession of him.

He had Monte Cristo's fortune. The fiction had become reality. It appeared to him pre-ordained. Travis' words of warning, his caution not to let the gold drag him down to the base level of dishonorable men, he had given little heed to, because they were a part of a story he had dismissed as fantasy. And they were not remembered now. They were swallowed in the mists. With the weapon of wealth hard in his hands, the picture of Amos Frost became the personification of Edmond Dante's enemies. The decision to avenge himself on Frost and his partners crystallized.

Mont Christian turned his back on the cave and led his laden mules down out of the haunted Sierra Madre del Norte.

CHAPTER
SIX

Amos Frost was in Goldfield, and so were the other three, Weldon Thomas, now with his own brokerage house, Arnold Hickman, a banker, James Farrel, owning the Buckeye Saloon. The San Francisco office of the Pinkerton Agency had taken only three days to locate them for Christian, since they were now prominent men and the town was the new magnet for everyone interested in mining. Now Christian was here too.

He had guessed wrong in telling Emma Bondford about the camp, that it was like all mining towns. Only Virginia City and Columbia in the old days equaled its glamor. He strolled the street that first night, wondering at the glitter, the demonstration of the wealth being given up by the ground here. The boat from Guaymas had disembarked him in San Francisco, the first city he had seen in fifteen years, but though it was larger and he had relished the lights and sounds and business, the Bay was now an international port with many interests.

In Goldfield there was only one topic of conversation on the streets — the mines. He stood on the corner of Crook Avenue and Main Street listening to the talk of the crowd that flowed around him, the gay noises that poured from the four saloons that faced on the intersection, the Palace, the Hermitage, the Mohawk and Tex Rickard's great Norther. Everyone in town, it seemed, must be on the streets that night.

He walked watchfully, looking into faces, looking for three faces in particular, but also for anyone he might recognize from Tombstone, flocking with everyone else to this new Mecca. Tonight was a test. He must show himself boldly and learn if Gilbert Lorran could still be known behind this thin face with the deep lines, beneath the groomed waves of white hair. On that would depend the pattern of his attack.

He did see men, faces he recalled, but even when he appeared to inadvertently jostle them they glanced at him once and then away. Except for one man. He was aware that he was being followed. Several times within the last two blocks he had turned casually to look back and found the same figure, hanging the same distance behind, swinging away quickly. He had not yet seen the man's face.

He stepped into the street and cut diagonally across and went into the Northern, shouldering without hurry toward the bar that stretched down the wall for sixty feet. Behind the polished counter a dozen barmen worked to keep pace with the demands of thirsty miners, gamblers, business men and visitors from all four corners of the earth.

Quietly he wedged in, others good humoredly making way for him, until he could look into the long backbar mirror, and was in time to see the batwing doors shoved open and his shadow step in and look hastily around. In relief he saw that it was Dick Butler, the gambler from the stage, and knew that this was no danger from his past.

He watched the man locate him, then angle on toward the gambling pit at the rear of the bar crowd and pass down its far side. The pit was a long rectangle fenced by rows of tables for craps, faro, blackjack and roulette, a sort of corral wherein a large crew of dealers in black clothes accommodated the throng that pressed three deep against the tables.

Butler disappeared from his sight, toward the poker lounge at the rear, and Christian forgot him as the bartender arrived. He asked for a bottle and glass, and when it was set before him poured a shot, full until it trembled above the rim. It pleased him that his hand was again so steady. He lifted it without spilling and drank it in a slow swallow, and then his body froze.

Wyatt Earp was pushing toward him along the bar. He set the glass down carefully, keeping his eyes on the mirror, in it watching the man with the sandy drooping mustache who had been marshal in Tombstone. It had not been Earp who had arrested him — he had been out of town at the time — but in a place the size of Tombstone they had seen each other often on the streets and in the saloons.

If Earp recognized the prisoner at large . . . There was nothing he could do, no place to turn, no way to hide his face, and then he smiled. He was not there to hide. He was Mont Christian, with a family Bible to prove it. He had found that down on lower Market Street, looking through second-hand stores for some sort of album on which to build a new identity. This one held old photographs and tintypes of round-headed, square-bearded men, of women with their hair pulled tight enough to make their eyes start out, a family from Utica, New York. The surname was not Christian, but as a given name it was used several times on the hand written page of the family's chronicle. He had no idea whether any of them still survived, but its being in that store made him guess that no one did. He had bought it, inscribed his name in ink mixed with dirt to simulate age, and built himself a background that would pass considerable challenge.

He did not turn as Earp approached, but in the mirror he saw the old marshal's eyes touch him, go over him with a quick, judging survey, and then pass on, as the man made his way to his office at the end of the bar.

Christian poured himself another drink, this time not so full, for in spite of the fact that Earp had not known him he was shaken. When the bartender came to collect he said idly,

"What's Earp doing in town?"

"Know him?" The man was courteous but not curious. "He's floor manager here. You new in Goldfield?"

"Got in today," Christian said. "Where's a good place to eat?"

"The Palm Grill." There was a civic pride in the voice. "Best restaurant this side of New York. No, damnit, the best in the country. Welcome to camp, Mr . . ."

"Christian. Mont Christian. Thanks, I'll be seeing you."

The bartender grinned at him with easy friendliness. "The name's Carl. Come back soon." He moved away to fill another order.

The street crowd was thick and colorful, with miners still in their working clothes, gentlemen in the newest fashions of the eastern cities, lean western men with the smell of horses about them, women as bright as tropical birds. The street lamps were dimmed by the brilliance flooding out from the long row of saloons, the gambling and dance halls. Christian passed the Mint, the Combination, the Phoenix, the Oriental, moving slowly, orienting himself, familiarizing himself with the town.

He turned in at the Palm Grill, a long room decorated with the spike-leaved plants in tubs, ornate and glittering and crowded. There was a clutch of people waiting inside the door and he paused with them. The head waiter spotted him at once and stepped toward him regally.

"Are you alone, sir?"

Christian nodded.

"It will be at least an hour before I can have a table for you. But if you don't mind sharing one . . ."

"Fine." Christian smiled at him.

The man led a winding course toward the rear of the room, to a table beneath a balcony on which a pianist and a violinist played a serenade that only they paid any attention to. A thin, boyish blond man sat there alone,

52

and the head waiter put his hands on the back of a second gilt chair, plainly expecting no objection.

"Billy, you don't mind if this gentleman joins you?"

The young man shook his head, swallowing a bite, his blue eyes open and inviting, filled with the friendliness that Christian thought was a special mark of the town. Perhaps, he thought, he noticed it because of its total absence through the long years of Yuma. Yet not everyone was a friend. As he took the chair that faced the front door he again saw Dick Butler, now waiting with the incoming diners, and knew that the man was following him, watching for the chance to even the score of the stage incident. He frowned, not liking the idea. He did not want his introduction on this scene to be an involvement with a fight.

The young man recalled his attention to the table, saying, "I'm Billy Murray, cashier at the Northern. I don't think I've seen you around."

"Mont Christian." It was becoming easier to say. "I'm a new boy."

Murray was red headed, Irish, and outgiving. He nodded vigorously. "The quail is good. Specialty of the house. But you can get anything here you can get in New York or Paris, if you can pay for it."

Christian glanced at the menu and thought of the high proportion of miners among the customers. "I see what you mean. How do the boys afford it?"

Murray chuckled, shaking his head in wonder. "Don't you worry about them. You never will see another town like this. They come off every eight-hour shift with from two hundred to two thousand dollars worth of hi-grade on them and rarin' to blow it."

Christian took it as a figure of speech. "Sounds like a pretty fair slice to take out of company ore."

"In the two years I've been at the Northern I've seen over seven million come through my cage. I didn't know there was that much money."

Now Christian felt that the boy was playing a game, testing a tenderfoot with a tall tale, and he had little interest. "Always is a little thieving going on, but anything like you're talking about the owners would put a stop to."

"So don't believe me. You'll find out." Murray was not offended. "But if you're interested in mining you'd be smart to listen."

"Okay, shoot." Christian's quail arrived, as delicate as promised, and he ate with pleasure, listening in growing belief and amazement.

"They can't afford to stop the stealing here," Murray said. "Most of the mines are being developed under short-term lease, say only six months, and trouble with the miners means loss of production. The ore in the Mohawk, for instance, is running better than twelve thousand dollars a ton. It's cheaper for the leaser to discount the hi-grading as long as ore is coming up. One of them cleared over four-hundred thousand last year, even after the thefts. It couldn't be done in Cripple Creek, for instance, because that was a complex ore, hard to recover the gold, but here it's free milling. All they have to do is break up the quartz and you've got practically pure metal."

"I can see that, but how do the miners get rid of it? You have to have a registered mine to ship to the mint."

"Assayers." Murray grinned. "There are seventy of them in Goldfield, and two thirds of them are nothing but fences. The miners wear a regular hi-grade vest that they can buy in the stores, like a big pocket. Some of the ore they drop in that runs ninety-percent gold. They come off shift and head for the assay office and take maybe a fifty-percent discount. Some of the assayers are making more than the mine owners."

"What about the foremen? Any kind of ore is bulky enough to be obvious."

The redhead was delighted with the extravagant outrage he watched daily. "Hell, man, the miners buy their jobs from the foremen, twenty dollars a day to hold a job that pays him four." His laughter rang out, almost girlish in its high hilarity.

Christian laughed with him. He was drawn to the boy's Irish gaiety, but he laughed for a different reason. He had not expected to find this easily a vulnerable point in Amos Frost; but Frost was an assayer and most probably deeply involved in buying stolen ore. It fitted neatly into his program.

He could not present the whole of Travis' ore for sale without there being questions asked as to where it had come from. He intended to open a mine here, no matter that it was worthless, build a small smelter and feed the Mexican gold into it as though it came from Goldfield's ground. If the product looked rich enough to Frost, perhaps the man could be drawn into a partnership that would begin his ruination.

Christian finished his dinner, paid his check, promised to see Murray again, and made his way to the street, thinking about Frost. Yet something at the back of his mind bothered him. He stopped on the sidewalk, opening himself to impressions, and became aware that Dick Butler was no longer in sight. Cautioned by this, he turned toward the hotel.

The street was still thronged. With three eight-hour shifts working in the mines, Goldfield apparently never went to bed. Women were more in evidence now, busy-eyed girls foraging among the crop of men, and Christian was not surprised to be stopped with an invitation.

"You'll like me," she said. "And I have a nice room." She was a tall blonde, almost as tall as he, with an overripe, maternal figure and a lonely emptiness behind large, liquid eyes.

"Not now, thanks," he said, and would have gone on, but she put a hand on his arm, tightening her fingers.

"I've got something special for you; you wouldn't want to miss it."

She pulled him, hauling him off balance so that he took two involuntary steps in surprise at her boldness on this bright main street. Then, when he tried to shake free, she argued.

A warning touched him, a note of urgency in her that was beyond the ordinary offering, and a suspicion made him smile.

"All right," he said, "let's go see. Which way?"

He thought there was relief in her as she turned toward the corner and led him with a long swinging stride down the dimmer cross street, talking constantly as if to hold his attention. That her name was Virginia was all he heard. He was busy watching the doorways as they passed, listening for footsteps behind them, expecting, as if he could see the arrangements being made, to find Butler following or lurking in wait.

Yet nothing happened. The crowd thinned and within two blocks there were only a few people on the sidewalk. It was darker here, the road lighted only by the shadow light of the desert stars. Christian walked easily, his muscles relaxed yet ready with the long habit of expecting sudden attacks from the companions of his prison cage. Since Butler was going to need to be handled, he was glad that it would come in an inconspicuous place.

And then another thought struck him. Perhaps it was not Butler. Perhaps Amos Frost had indeed recognized him, had quietly set a trap, an ambush for him. Of one thing he was sure. He was not being led along this way by this girl on her usual errand.

If it were Butler, well and good. If it were Frost, he must learn that the man was alerted, but why should he go to this trouble when he had only to expose Gilbert Lorran to the authorities? Puzzling this, he checked that his gun hung freely in its holster and went on, but even more watchful now.

The alley mouth appeared abruptly, hidden between two houses that seemed almost too close together to permit a passage. Virginia tugged on his arm again as they came abreast the dark mouth, trying to center his attention on her, and he felt his pulse quicken. So the danger waited there. She did not try to turn him into the alley where he could be rushed. This suggested a gun, a shot from an unseen assailant. Suddenly the girl stumbled and bent down, as if her shoe had turned.

All of these things Christian made note of in the same instant, the instant it took him to put one hand on her hip and shove her sprawling in the street, to pull his gun and fling himself prone toward the deep shade of the yawning slot.

A shot answered his lunge, its aim spoiled by his surprise move, the bright flash from the gun giving him a target, closer than he had expected.

Christian held his own fire. He did not want to kill the attacker. He wanted him alive, talking. He rolled forward, pulled his feet up under him and crouched, preparing to spring toward his target. But his foot struck a discarded bottle and sent it clattering against the rubble on the alley floor, and the man waiting for him ran.

Christian jumped, following the echoing footsteps, unable to see what was ahead or underfoot, hearing the man stumble against obstacles. He himself came against a barrel, hard, sidestepped and fell headlong over a large box. Then in the darkness he heard a crash and a grunt as the wind was knocked out of the other. Mont was on him like a panther, his feet locating the body as it would struggle up, his hand dropping the gun into its place. His fingers swept across the figure, searching over the legs, the trunk, finding the throat. He grappled it in one hand and slammed his other fist into the yielding face.

There was a gasp, then thick legs wrapped around his middle and rolled him back. He lost his grip and felt the other come up and butt him, but the blow struck his shoulder and did him no harm. The man found his feet and ran again, coming into the far end of the alley where more light filtered through.

Christian raced after him, careless of his footing, and dived on the dark back still twenty feet short of the street. They went down together, and now Christian could distinguish the thrashing legs and arms. He felt first for the thick waist and found no gun belt, then the barrel of the weapon he was hunting came down on his crown, sending a burst of flashing light spots shooting through his head.

He reached for the arm, found it and threw his weight on it, carrying it down to jar against the hard ground, and he felt the gun glance off his hand as it spun away. A fist caught him on his cheek and legs sought to tangle him again. He brought up a knee swiftly, low in the soft stomach and felt the convulsive doubling of the body. Then kneeling, he locked his fingers in the trousers and in the shirt near the neck. He lifted the body and slammed it back to earth. Heavy breath rushed from the other's throat and for a moment he lay still.

In that moment Christian caught him by his coat and shirt and hauled him up to a sitting position first and then with a twisting lurch brought him to his feet. The man flailed, throwing two quick punches that found their mark in Christian's stomach, sickening him. Christian whirled him around, bent him backward and threw a paralyzing blow against the side of the neck. The figure slumped in his grasp. Christian turned him to full face again, yanked, and pulled him across the narrow alley. The man came with little running steps and Christian used the momentum to hurl him against the wall. He held him there with one hand and with the other slashed his fist again and again into the face until the head rolled forward, loose with unconsciousness.

Christian lowered him into a heap, only then becoming aware that his lungs were on fire, that his breath came in ragged gasps. He felt an astringent shrinking inside his head and knew that the old wildness of his early prison days had broken free again, that if the other had not passed out he might have killed him. The thought brought him a chill. He had believed that he had controlled that dormant explosiveness.

He shook his head, waiting for his senses to clear, and then stooped, caught the man up again and dragged him close enough to the alley mouth to see the face. It was beaten raw, bleeding and beginning to swell, but recognizable as Dick Butler.

That was a relief at least. Christian rose to his feet and turned to leave, but then swung back as a new possibility occurred. Butler was a coward, an assassin who shot from hiding and ran when physical violence threatened. He was a gambler, known and noted in the camp as dangerous and a bully. Mont Christian had, he decided, a use for such a creature.

Slowly, as a lion approaches the raw carcass that will be its dinner, he squatted down, shaking the limp shoulder, calling Butler's name softly.

The eyes opened finally, glazed but gradually clearing. They widened as they saw the white hair of the head above them, the hungry smile bent upon them, and the body shrunk tighter against the ground.

Christian said in a quiet voice, in which there was no hint of feeling, "Now let's go and get a little better acquainted. Just keep still and you won't get hurt."

Butler lay without sound, staring upward. Christian lifted him to his feet, slung one arm around his own shoulder and supported him, walking him as if he were drunk, out onto the side street. He turned away from the main artery and found a route down the dim rear road to the back entrance of the hotel.

The kitchens were in the basement, he found, and the service stairs went directly up. He had an explanation ready, that he had found Butler outside, but he had no need to use it. He saw no one as he more than half carried the man up to his room. In the hall he propped Butler against the wall, found his key and opened the door and brought the man inside, dropping him into a chair. He brought a wet towel from the bathroom, sponged the bruised face until the dulled senses sharpened, until Butler straightened and looked at him in blank bewilderment. Then he brought up another straight-backed chair, reversed it and sat down, folding his arms along the top rung and resting his chin on them, his face close to Butler's. He showed no anger, no sign that they had so recently fought so savagely. Instead, he looked amused.

"Now," he said, "I think that we can make some money together, a lot of money." He waited a moment while the words registered through the dazed brain, and then added, "Just as long as you understand that you wear my brand. If you forget, don't let me find you again. How does it sound?"

He had, he saw, judged his man right. Avarice took the place of bewilderment. Fear gave way to an opportunist's acceptance of a fate that promised profit.

Slowly Butler extended his hand and made an attempt at a heavy smile.

"You call the shots, mister," he said. "I guess I'd rather be on your side."

CHAPTER
SEVEN

Whatever Dick Butler expected of his new employment, it was not the delay, the waiting, the uncertainty
that ran on and frustrated him and puzzled him while
Mont Christian sat idle, watching Goldfield, learning it.

Never had Christian pictured such a town. Set in the
stretch of barren desert that flanks the upper half of the
notorious Death Valley, it was isolated from all refining
forces of civilization, making its own rules to govern the
wildest collection of human beings who could be found
gathered into one locality.

Within two years of the day when two partners
labored to open their claim on a grub stake so meager
that they lived on a single meal from sunup to sunup,
the town roared into a city of twenty-five thousand
souls. Miners stole an estimated quarter of a million
dollars a day and spent their tarnished fortunes in the
two hundred saloons, the gambling houses and the red
light district that mushroomed to serve them.

The flow of stolen gold alone would have supported
the average businesses of a town ten times the size.
Pimps, con men, whores, flooded in from the Barbary
Coast, from Alaska, from Denver's Tenderloin, from the

Seattle waterfront and from the dying Colorado silver camps, all attracted by the easy dollars.

Syndicates of eastern millionaires; Schwab, Lowden, Carnegie, vied with each other to buy up the mines. Such local magnates as L. L. Patrick, Al Meyers, Tasker Oddie, George Nixon and Winfield poured their vast profits back into the camp. A hundred brokerage houses, members of the Goldfield Stock Exchange, sold shares in the booming mines through every city in the country and half the capitals of Europe. Local newspapers ran dire stories which were reprinted across the world carrying the warning that the flow of yellow metal threatened the monetary structure of the globe, arguing that gold would be over-produced and become as cheap as iron or lead.

It was a wild time, an insane town, and its extravagance exactly suited Mont Christian's mood. In his own eyes Gilbert Lorran was a dead man walking among the living. He was a ghost returned to lead to destruction those who had destroyed him. He had no other interest. The goals that spur living men on to great endeavor did not stir him. He existed solely for vengeance, unheeding the fortunes made so carelessly around him.

Any man with a strong back and a willingness to work could have from any mine owner a lease on ten feet of ground. It was a cheap way of developing a mine to the point where it would interest an eastern capitalist.

Dick Butler brought a tale of one such man who walked into town with empty pockets, not even the price of a pick, was given a lease on the Mohawk, borrowed tools and dug three hundred tons of ore that averaged twenty-two hundred dollars to the ton, then sold his lease to Patrick for ten thousand down and twenty percent of all that could be taken from the tunnel within six months.

Such stories were common, but none of them quickened Christian's excitement. To his mind the gold he had brought from Mexico was enough for his purpose. Yet he was pleased to hear them, for they established a climate that favored his ends.

Having put off his own name and assumed the new identity, his next aim was that this identity should win the confidence and arouse the greedy instinct of Amos Frost and his associates. Just as Monte Cristo had used the greed of his enemies to lead them to their disasters, so Mont Christian meant to deal with those who had cost him so dearly.

To this end he opened an office in the building next to the Northern saloon, and through Dick Butler saw that it was noised across the camp that he was a mining man who had struck it rich in Mexico and was now looking for local investments. It was bait to draw one of Frost's crowd forward, but although many offers of deals were made, none came from the people he sought. Frost ignored him. True, he met the assayer from time to time in one of the bars. Frost was always pleasant, but nothing more.

Time drew out. Christian's early expectations settled into patient waiting. Prison teaches a man patience.

Within a month Butler had brought him a dozen proposals, and to each he had shaken his head.

Butler grew bewildered and restless, unable to comprehend why his employer was paying him five hundred a month and apparently using none of his talents. He guessed that Christian had some plan, but he could not ferret it out, and mysteries made him uneasy.

Out of his gnawing dissatisfaction he complained. "I don't get it. What are you looking for? I don't see what you're sitting around waiting on. Why don't we get moving?"

Christian eyed him coldly. He did not like his henchman and made no effort to dissemble. "What's bothering you? You're getting paid, aren't you?"

"Well, yes" — the heavy-set man shifted under the direct stare — "but I like to see what I'm getting into. Besides, people are beginning to talk, ask questions; they're curious who you are and why you're here."

It was a development that Christian did not like. He had not supposed that Goldfield had the time to indulge in curiosity, and he did not want any probing, any mystery to grow. He shrugged carelessly.

"I've told you, I'm looking for a mine. Tell them that."

"I have. And I've brought you chance after chance. What the hell do you want?"

"A good claim. Have you brought me a good one?"

Butler moved his thick shoulders and turned sullen. "How do I know if they're good? Gold is where you find it. If you're a mining man you ought to know that."

Christian gave him a thin smile. "I promised you I'd make you money, and a lot. I'll do it my way and in my time. If, that is, you stand hitched. Now get out of here. Get drunk or do whatever you like. When I'm ready we'll go to work."

He watched the man go and knew that Butler was not satisfied, and knew also that he could wait no longer. He had searched quietly for any weakness among the Frost crowd and found nothing that he might turn to his advantage, nor had they approached him. He was forced to take the initiative now, to make the move that he had so far put off and kept as an alternate entry.

That evening, with a box of candy beneath his arm, Mont Christian paid a call on Emma Bondford, approaching for the first time the house that Amos Frost had built for himself on the rising flank of Columbia mountain.

Emma Bondford was a strong woman, not helpless, but being untrained and unfamiliar with the rough country, she did not know which way to turn. There were few jobs for such as she in Goldfield. She could not sew well enough to become a milliner or dressmaker; she did not know how to wait table; and even the public schools were closed to her, for she had no credentials of a formal education. So she had crowded down her anger at Frost's surly manner towards her, had put up with the unruliness of the children and was indeed becoming fond of them. She was desperately hoarding every dollar of her salary, building a stake that could one day take her back East or at least to one of the Pacific coast cities.

But meanwhile the loneliness oppressed her. She welcomed Christian's call with embarrassing gratitude that anyone in this brawling town should realize she was alive.

On his part, Christian set himself to win the girl's confidence. It was not hard to penetrate her reticence, to start her talking of her problems, for she needed to talk. He understood the loneliness and used it to his advantage. She was inside the enemy camp. She was his passport to Amos Frost's stronghold.

His first call was short. On later evenings he lingered, spending an hour or two at the house. He became a regular visitor. Coolly he decided that it was best not to meet Frost within his own walls, and chose his times when he knew the man was in town. Besides the regular gift of candy for Emma Bondford he unfailingly brought trinkets for the children, and soon they would wait for him in the yard. He courted them as he would court a coyote puppy in the hills until their brash curiosity broke through the restraints of Emma's and the housekeeper María's stern warnings against asking questions.

"How many men did you shoot in Mexico?"

It was the boy, sitting crosslegged on the porch at his feet one warm evening. Peggy was perched on Christian's knee and Emma Bondford leaned comfortably against the railing. Christian smiled at her quick frown and winked at her.

68

"Not many, Amos. What makes you think I shot any?"

"Papa says you did."

Emma Bondford said sharply, "Amos, that is not true. What your father said, and he was joking, was that Mr. Christian looked like a gunfighter, that he walked like one, and that judging by the friends he chose in Goldfield he probably was one." It cost her a blush to say so much on so intimate a subject, but her own uneasiness over the suspicion needed an answer. Yet Christian turned the direct question aside with a light laugh.

"What friends would those be?"

"Dick Butler, for one," she pushed on now. "After you put him off the stage that day I would have thought he would hate you, and you despise him."

To her surprise he simply shrugged.

"Dick's not so bad when he's sober. I need someone to run errands, and to laugh at now and then."

And that was all the answer they had that night.

CHAPTER
EIGHT

In her own room Emma Bondford stood before the dresser mirror alternately examining herself cirtically and asking herself riddles that went round and round without answers.

How much longer could she remain in the Frost house? How long could she endure Goldfield. She was seized with homesickness for the spreading waters of Lake Michigan, for the fresh air, the bustle of the Loop, for the friends with whom she had grown up.

After her father's death she had deliberately cut herself away from them all, and had not written a single letter since coming west. In growing distress she thought that there was not a person in the world with the exception of Mont Christian who cared whether she lived or died. And she was not at all certain that he cared. Nor that she wanted him to.

He came to the house now at least four nights a week, but he showed more interest in the Frost children that he did in her. Never by the slightest sign had he indicated that he saw her as a desirable woman. Instead, there was something withdrawn about him, as if he were afraid of her, or as if he had some secret to hide. Not once had he referred to a family or friends.

Never had he said where he was born or what his father did. It was not natural.

Several times she had caught herself telling about her own childhood, about her mother who had died when she was ten. One evening she had been astonished to find herself talking about her father's suicide, although she had been unable to mention it aloud until then. There was a way Christian had of drawing out her deepest thoughts.

He had listened to the tragedy with his detached sympathy, yet even that recital had brought no return confidence from him. It was as if he had not existed before the day he had stepped into the Sodaville stage.

He was more open with the children than he was with her. To them he told wonderful stories. Even so, he never put himself into them. It was always about some other man, something someone had told him about the early mining days, or the Indians across the border, or the first Spanish explorers. In fact the boy and girl monopolized him most of the time, and it was a joy how a single word from him could make them mind. Even María blossomed when Christian was around, principally, Emma thought, because he spoke to her in her own language.

María was trying to promote a romance. "He is a good man," she insisted. "Me, I know. I have known many men."

Fat, shapeless, her copper face hanging in jowls, it seemed incredible to Emma that any man could have looked with passion upon the woman; still she spoke with confidence.

"He is not bad. He has been hurt. It is in his face and in his way. He trusts no one but the children. The children cannot hurt him."

"But why does he come to see me? He doesn't even talk like the men I knew in the East."

"He comes." The housekeeper lifted her heavy shoulders. "Marry him. It is said in town that he is very rich."

"They also whisper that he's a killer. I saw his gun once, under his vest."

"He could kill, yes, someone in his way. But he is not a brute. You marry him and you can go away from this house and the spider man who owns it."

It was the first time María had mentioned any opinion of her employer. Emma had supposed that she merely accepted him mindlessly.

"You don't like Mr. Frost?"

"No more than you. The money is good. But the man is like a snake, scheming, figuring, figuring. I would not trust him with a dollar of mine."

María had cleared away the tea things left from Christian's visit and departed to the kitchen, and the homesickness had struck Emma Bondford like an engulfing wave, for the idea of marrying the white-haired man was something new, something she had not considered. So she had hurried to her room and the confrontation with the mirror.

If she married Christian, yes, she could escape from Frost's house. But would she escape the raw life of the mining town? Who was Christian? What kind of man was he really? What did he actually do? How much money did he really have and what stains were on it? Did he have dreams, plans, hopes? His view of the future was as dark to her as his past. On these puzzles she spent a restless night.

Emma Bondford was not the only person concentrating on Mont Christian that warm summer evening. Amos Frost was thinking about the man very carefully as he sat in the rear room of Sally Ringe's Miners' Bar on Ore Street.

It was Sally's boast that she was well acquainted with every important man in Goldfield; yet she had bowed to Frost's demand when Christian came to town.

"Keep away from him until I find out about him," the assayer had said.

Now she knew that Christian was bothering him. Frost sat looking at her but not seeing the pleasant features, the wide, warm appearing mouth, or the give-away eyes, gray and shiny as wet slate.

Large, big busted, her waist tightly corseted into a semblance of slimness, Sally Ringe was to be reckoned with in camp for assets other than her size. She had power, although no one knew its source, and a dozen men who would do her bidding for a price made the saloon their headquarters. The town had wondered for two years at her relationship with Amos Frost. Some guessed that Frost was the secret owner of the establishment, but if so it was known only to the two principals. Otherwise the relationship was plain to see, for Frost spent much more time in her company than he did at his home.

He stared through her and twisted a brandy glass in his surprisingly strong fingers. He was a soft looking, baby-faced man, his red lips pouting and damply glistening. His beard was so fine that it hardly showed against his smooth cheeks, his eyebrows and hair were so light as to seem only a layer of the white, unhealthy skin. Many people had wondered what a woman of Sally's strong appetites found attractive in this man. Only the light-pupiled eyes, boring into one, held command and domination. He focused them in on the woman.

"I don't figure this Christian." His tone was moody. "I can't learn a thing about him. My men tracked him back to San Francisco, he came in there on a boat from Guaymas, but my inquiries in Mexico drew a blank. No one at any of the mining centers down there knew him."

Sally arched an eyebrow. Knowing that Frost kept a group of private agents to gather a history of every man in camp who showed promise of any success, she was mildly amused at their failure to trace Christian.

"He's probably a nobody, just blown into Goldfield to pick up an easy buck, a slicker." Sally was an old hand at mining camps, prominent in Central City, Leadville, Cripple Creek, the Idaho camps, and over the Yukon trail. "Forget him until he starts being a nuisance, if he does."

Frost shook his head in dissatisfaction. "I've got a hunch about him. There's something I can't quite place. He may be a Pinkerton man sent in to check on the hi-grading. There's some talk that Winfield and Nixon want to get the mine owners together to try to stop it."

Sally's amusement turned to alarm. A good twenty-percent of the gold stolen from the mines along the reef filtered through Amos Frost's hands. His was a close-knit organization shared by his partners, Weldon Thomas, who owned a small bank, Arnold Hickman, a partner in a large brokerage house that was a member of the stock exchange and so in a position to execute the buying and selling orders of the group's trade in local stocks, and James Farrel. Farrel operated the Buckeye Saloon and Gambling Parlor, not as big a place as the Northern or the Mint, but catering to working miners, the hi-graders.

It was in one or another of the Buckeye's gambling rooms that the deals were made whereby a house messenger would carry the stolen ore to the rear door of Frost's assay office. No such illicit traffic was ever handled over the office counter, and Frost's reputation among the businessmen was without reproach. The illegal horde was simply spirited through Thomas' bank or into the stock market via Arnold Hickman.

Even Sally did not know the extent of Frost's wealth. He took no one into full confidence, but her educated guess after watching for two years was that Frost's share must amount to over three million, and such a sum staggered her, as conditioned as she was to Goldfield's enormous figures.

Under this possible threat of prying she laid a jeweled hand over his.

"Amos, why don't we quit while we're ahead and safe?"

He looked startled, then his odd-colored, lizard eyes narrowed. "While we're sitting on top of the biggest pile of gold on earth? Don't be stupid."

"It won't do you much good if the Pinkertons catch on and send you to Carson City for ten or twenty years."

He sneered at her. "You're a coward. They couldn't get any proof in a thousand years."

"Then why are you worried about this Christian?"

He shook off her hand in uneasy impatience. "I just don't like him nosing around."

Her shoulder moved casually. "I can have him drygulched for a hundred bucks, and no questions."

There was a sourness in his tone. "It may come to that, but not yet. I want to make sure who's behind him first. No point in killing one man if they'll just put another on my heels. It's easier to watch Christian."

"He's hired Dick Butler, you know."

"Of course I know. He probably thought Butler was thick with the local thieves and would finger them for him. But Butler's a blowhard. No one in his right mind would tell him a thing."

She said cautiously, not wanting him to see her interest, "Do you want me to work on Christian? Men tell me things, you know."

76

His face puckered. "Too obvious, if he's smart. But I think another way is ripe. Christian has been making up to that girl I hired to teach the kids. I've been watching. I don't think he's interested in her, I think he's trying to get at me through her. Tomorrow night I'm going to learn. I'm going to insult her enough that she'll leave. And I want you to have Pie Berman staked out."

Frost felt sure of Berman. The bouncer at the bar was a tough, a one-time sailor who in a saloon brawl in Alaska had killed a camp favorite. Sally Ringe had saved him from a noose, and he had followed her slavishly ever since, slow-witted, brutal, loyal.

"Get it through his skull that I don't want her really hurt. Tell him to pick a dark spot, grab her, snatch her purse and rough her up a little. When he lets her go she'll head straight for Christian. She hasn't got another friend in town."

The idea pleased Sally. She was jealous of Emma Bondford, not physically, for she knew that she could give a man much more than the eastern girl would even comprehend. But in her heart she dreamed of marrying Frost and raising his children, and so long as the governess was in his house he had no need of Sally there. Yet she could not see the motive behind Frost's present plan.

"And what's that going to show you?"

"Use your head. If Christian is sweet on the girl he'll keep her away from my place, but if he's using her to snoop he'll talk her into coming back. Then we'll know."

Sally Ringe relaxed audibly. "Damnit, Amos, I'm glad I don't have to play poker with you. I never met anybody any sharper in the brain."

And Frost relaxed then too, under her unaccustomed flattery.

CHAPTER
NINE

Mont Christian was entertaining a visitor in his hotel room the following night. The man, the same operative who had located Amos Frost and his associates for the client, was saying;

"The old man thought you ought to know. Frost's agents have been asking a lot of questions about you in San Francisco."

That Frost might suspect him brought Christian sharply alert.

"What kind of questions?"

The man's eyes glowed with caustic humor. "Pretty shrewd ones, by and large. But we got the idea they think you're one of our agents."

Christian gaped at him, and then laughed aloud. That was the last answer he had expected. The agent looked at him curiously. He did not know why Mont Christian had wanted to locate Frost, but the agency had been paid handsomely, and it was a rule of the Pinkerton office to protect a client.

"We thought you might be interested."

"Indeed I am," Christian sobered. It annoyed him that even the Pinkertons knew that he had hunted Amos Frost, but there was no help for it. It had been the only way he knew of finding the man without months or years of searching. "Thanks, and tell the chief to send a bill."

The operative nodded and rose, and when he had gone Christian poured himself a careful drink. He seldom drank alone, but this disclosure that despite Frost's apparent indifference to him he had been actively investigating called for consideration, and a little alcohol could ease his tension, free his thinking. If Frost was interested and yet avoiding any contact, then it was surely time that Christian must find a more direct method of forcing some move by Frost. The waiting, even the long vigil at the house, had not turned the trick.

He discarded one notion and then another and was still seeking a method when a bellboy knocked at his door, calling through it.

"There's a woman downstairs asking for you."

"A woman?" Christian was startled. "What kind of a woman?"

The boy was knowledgeable. Enough girls spent the night in the guests' rooms that he had learned to tell the difference.

"A lady, sir. Her face is dirtied up and her dress is torn. She seems to be in trouble."

Christian, descending the stairs, saw Emma Bondford huddled in a deep chair, her hair awry and a bruise swelling beneath her left eye. As she rose uncertainly he saw the rent where one shoulder of her dress had been torn nearly out of its eye.

"In God's name," he said, "what happened to you?" He took her arm and pressed her again into the chair, bending above her.

She was not crying. She had never permitted herself many tears. But her voice was ragged.

"Everything happened. That Frost man, he really is a devil. He came home for supper nastier than usual. He started to taunt me, said I wasn't a real woman or I'd catch myself a man instead of staying there letting myself be kicked around by kids I couldn't control. He kept on until I couldn't take any more. I resigned. He bet me I'd be back in the morning. I got my things and started down the street. I had nearly ninety dollars in my purse, and I was going to San Francisco. But in the dark a man grabbed me. He forced his mouth against mine. He smelled of whiskey. Then he started to rip off my dress. I fought him and he hit me in the face and knocked me down. When I got up he had run with my bag and my purse."

She looked up at him, her eyes asking forgiveness. "I didn't know what to do except to come here and ask for you."

"You did perfectly right. I'll get you a room; then in the morning I'll put you on the stage for anywhere you choose. You aren't hurt otherwise?"

"No, I'm all right. But now I haven't any money, not a cent."

He smiled encouragement. "Money is the least important thing in the world unless you haven't any. It so happens that I have quite a deal of it. Don't worry."

But her misery did not lift. Instead she looked trapped and her words sounded foolish.

"But I can't take any from you."

Christian's patience began to slip. Such an emergency was not a time to stand on social mores.

"Call it a loan," he said. "Let's not be silly; you can't walk to Sodaville."

Now he thought that she would cry. "I know . . . but I . . ."

"You're upset." He spoke as if she were a child. "It's no wonder, but let's not argue tonight. A night's sleep here will make things look simpler in the morning."

But the trapped look only increased, and she shook her head sharply. "I just cannot borrow from you."

He had not found her stupid before, and puzzlement increased his impatience so that he said roughly, "Then what did you come here for?"

"I don't know . . . I don't know." The voice was a wail and her head dropped so that he could not see her face. "Don't you understand, you're the last person in the world I could take money from."

He caught his breath, unable to believe what he knew she meant until she raised her head and he saw the softness in her eyes. In his own mind he was a broken man, white haired, his face deeply etched. That a woman could want him he could not comprehend. Yet this was plainly written on her now, and yet alone here, without experience, she still had the pride to refuse his help.

Emotion, that he had believed dead, warmed in him, warmed toward her. But he took it for pity and crowded it down. There was no room in his life for pity any longer, and he forced himself to speak casually.

"If you won't borrow from me, where do you expect to turn?"

She was thinking more clearly now. His very presence, his offer of aid, and her sure new knowledge of her own feelings had driven off some of her doubts.

"I'll go back to the Frost house. I should not have given way and left. It was very childish."

"You would do that?"

She moved her shoulders wearily. "He doesn't mean half he says. There's good in him; it shows when he's with the children. I think he's unsure, somehow, and takes it out in embarrassing other people. I'll go back and stay until I can save enough to leave Goldfield."

That, he thought, would be best for both of them, that she leave. There was no place for a woman in his plans, nor did he want the affection she had showed him to grow stronger. She should not be needlessly hurt. But he watched with an odd reluctance until she lifted her chin and said levelly,

"I should have learned by now not to let my temper get away from me, and I will learn by my mistake. Would you be kind enough to walk me back there? I won't be easy on a dark street alone again."

He gave her his hand without speaking and drew her from the chair, but as they crossed the lobby the cautious glances of the clerks and loiterers warned him that the story, in some garbled form, would spread across Goldfield the next day. It did not matter. In fact, as a small irony that might discomfit Frost, he thought to add a little fuel.

As they passed the Palm Grill he turned her toward the door.

"A little food will refresh you. The oysters here are famous, and the quail is the best."

She looked at the bright window. It would be good to again go somewhere in the evening where there was laughter and human companionship, but she drew back.

"Not tonight, not bedraggled as I am."

If she hoped he would suggest another time he disappointed her. He did not press, and they went on.

On the dark road up the hill she paused, pointing out a spot between two buildings, saying, "This is where the man jumped me."

Christian looked at the row of single-storied frame buildings and the black mouth of the alley, then struck a match and stepped into the gloom. A few feet inside he found the girl's bag and brought it back.

"Here's this, at least. I didn't find your purse."

She was immensely relieved, even finding a small smile. "Don't say 'at least' — all the clothes I own are in there. This will help a lot, thank you."

The light was burning in the hall of the Frost house and Emma Bondford let herself in quietly. An hour later Amos Frost paused on the walk, smiling sardonically as he looked at the lighted upstairs window.

Apparently the man who called himself Christian had sent her back, and Amos took his point for proven.

Christian would bear closer watching and more diligent investigation. Perhaps he would need to get rid of the man eventually.

CHAPTER
TEN

Amos Frost had further confirmation of his fears in the morning. Five of the hotel employees were in his pay, and there was a report of Emma Bondford's disheveled visit there waiting in his office. With it was the notation of Christian's earlier caller, recognized by a bellhop who had worked in the San Francisco Palace as an operative of the Pinkerton Detective Agency.

So Christian had been sent to Goldfield to spy upon Frost. At least Frost now knew who he was, and that to have him killed would only bring another quiet figure to continue the work. Yet the agent must be made ineffective somehow.

First, he decided, he must buy Dick Butler. Butler was not the type to stay loyal; he would cheerfully take Christian's money and inform on him to anyone who offered enough more. But Frost did not want to approach Butler personally, that was a job for James Farrel. The saloonkeeper could make the arrangement without arousing Butler's suspicion that Frost was behind the inquiries.

So it was no accident when, as Butler dropped into the Buckeye that afternoon on his daily rounds of the gambling houses, he found Farrel behind the bar and in a pleasant mood, offering a drink on the house.

"A man gets dry, even on this side of the counter."

Butler agreed with alacrity and Farrel shoved the bottle toward him, confiding,

"It ain't often I indulge in midday, but once in awhile I get a sadness in me for the old country, and nothing heals it but the whiskey. And I don't like to drink alone."

Dick Butler had never been known to refuse free whiskey. He poured a second glass, eyeing Farrel without appearing to. For all his bluster the gambler had a native shrewdness, and this uncommon gesture warned him that Farrel wanted something other than a drinking companion. He was ready when in the next moment Farrel said idly;

"Talk is you're working for this new man, Mont Christian."

"That's right." Butler grinned broadly.

"Seems like I see you around town a lot. From the looks, it don't seem he keeps you too busy."

Butler yawned to show his lack of interest. "He don't, really. He's a man takes his time looking around."

"What's he looking for?"

"A mine, or a lease. A lot of people have made him offers but he ain't settled on anything yet."

"He'd better move fast." Farrel poured another glass. "At the rate people are coming in the good ground will all be took up soon."

Butler had no trouble dissembling here. "That's what I try to tell him, but he ain't an easy man to convince."

"He's got people plumb curious about him," Farrel mused. "There's some would pay a piece of change for a bit of information."

Dick Butler's hand trembled slightly as he poured another drink, uninvited. "How big a piece of change?"

Farrel appeared to hesitate. "Depends on the information, like where he comes from, or how much money he's got, or if he buys a mine."

Butler shrugged casually. "He don't say where he's from. He's real close-mouthed, like maybe he's hiding out from something. As far as his money, you got me there. He's got enough, pays my wages in gold, not by check. As for a mine, if he has one I don't know it."

Farrel hid his disappointment but kept trying. "He wouldn't be working for some big company, some of them eastern millionaires, maybe?"

"Never heard a word to make me believe it."

"Well, if you hear anything that's interesting you'll know who to tell."

"Could be," said Dick Butler.

"And I wouldn't want Christian to get the idea I'm at all curious." Farrel drew five twenty-dollar gold pieces from his pocket and stacked them neatly before Butler. "That's just to make sure he don't hear. There's more, a lot more, where this comes from."

Butler eyed the coins with a simulated reluctance, then slowly palmed them, finished his drink and grinned.

"I'll be back, friend."

After he had gone Farrel sent a note to Amos Frost, an innocent note that would mean nothing of import if the messenger chose to sneak a look at it.

Dick Butler made a circuitous way to the office Christian had rented down street from the hotel, and wandered in. There was no one in the outer room, but Mont Christian was at the desk inside, reading a copy of the Goldfield News. Butler slouched into a chair without removing his hat and said without greeting;

"I just made a hundred bucks." He told the story not out of loyalty but in the hope of playing gain against gain. "Jim Farrel down at the Buckeye wants to know things about you. He give me the hundred not to tell you he was asking."

Christian laid the paper down slowly, saying without emphasis, "Why are you telling me?"

Butler pulled his hat from his head and stared into the dented crown as if to find an answer there.

"Ah, hell, I'm working for you, ain't I? You know I wouldn't talk about your business."

Christian's thin smile told Butler how deep was his employer's trust, then Christian said pleasantly;

"Even if I wanted you to?"

The gambler's eye came up quickly and gained a trace of cunning. "Meaning?"

"We'll get further if you don't try to second guess me."

Butler managed to look hurt. "Is that a way to talk when I'm just trying to help you?"

Christian stood up and leaned across the desk, his eyes on Butler, hard, his lips tight.

"Friend Dick," he said, "you are not trying to help me. You never tried to help anyone in your miserable life, so let's not pretend. You want to help Dick Butler. I told you I'd make you money and I will, a lot of money, more than you ever dreamed of. But I'll take no foolishness from you nor from anyone else."

He paused to give weight to his next words. "You do as I tell you, repeat nothing of my business to anyone unless I say to, and we'll get along. Cross me and I'll kill you as quick as I'd step on a snake."

Butler jerked as if he had been physically hit, and Christian went on.

"All right. Now, who do you figure Farrel wanted the information for?"

Butler wet his lips. This part he had intended to keep to himself for future use, but now he did not dare.

"If you ask me, it's the assayer, Frost."

"What makes you say that?"

"You hear things at a gambling table. I know that if a man has gold to sell he don't go to Frost's office, he goes to the back room at the Buckeye."

"How widely is this known?"

Butler crawfished. "Well, I don't know it for certain, I just suspect. It ain't healthy to know too much about Amos Frost. There was a man last year, a miner, got liquored and bragged that he knew who was behind the gold stealing and that he could prove it. Three days later he was dead."

Mont Christian sat back in his chair with a languorous movement, looking at Butler. He wondered if, had he questioned the man in the beginning, he would have got this simple answer. Had he needlessly wasted all this time? No, he decided. He knew a great deal more about the town than he had then. And now, he felt, it was time. It was time. Dick Butler thought his employer's smile looked more like a hungry wolf's than ever.

"Let's go to work," Christian said suddenly. "Let's go get us a mine."

"Just like that, huh? Just go out and get a mine."

"Why not?"

"Hell," Butler was puzzled and now disgusted. "Men have used up their lives looking for a paying property. All the good ground is taken or leased, and there's a thousand prospectors out in the brush breaking their hearts scrabbling and not finding anything worth digging."

"They aren't me." Christian's smile widened. "I have what is known as a nose for ore. Clear out of here now, and meet me in the hotel dining room at nine tomorrow morning."

He watched Butler go and continued to sit, feeling an electric charge start through him, a building of some semblance of excitement that the end of waiting was here, that now he could set the wheels of his vengeance in motion.

Later he rose and went to the hotel and climbed to his room. He had had a special lock put on the door, one that only he could open, and had established the practice of allowing the maid inside only when he was present. During these times he would sit on the two heavy boxes over which he had draped a large Spanish shawl.

He threw the shawl aside, unlocked and opened the box lids and lifted out the layer of clothes. Beneath them in each box was a solid bottom, but he fitted a knife blade into the tiny slots of these, drew out the false floors and exposed the leather sacks below. There, safely, reposed the gold dust that he had brought from Mexico.

He picked up one sack, examining it, assuring himself that the horsehair noose tied around its neck was undisturbed. It was a ritual that he performed at least twice a day, standing, looking down on the wealth, seeing in it not something he possessed but rather the tool by which he would settle scores with Amos Frost, Thomas, and Hickman.

Dick Butler might only suspect Frost's involvement with the hi-grading, but to Christian it had the ring of truth, and Frost's misstep in trying to use Butler against him, through the Buckeye contact, was all Christian needed to prove to him that the assayer had not changed his ways, that he could still be attacked through the lure of gold.

Much of his plan must be left to opportunism, according to what avenues Frost himself opened, what situations afforded themselves. But Christian could make his first move confidently now.

He must acquire a small mine. He did not expect to find a property of any value. He would build a small mill and salt his ground with the Mexican dust. He would establish himself as owner of a producing claim and then give them the opportunity to try to take it from him. Let them try. Let their foot slip, as it must if he were alert. Then he could bring them crashing down, their carefully built reputations and fortunes on top of them.

At eight o'clock the next morning he was breakfasting in the coffee shop, looking not at all like a man intent on finding a mine. Rather he looked like a gambler. His long broadcloth coat was expertly cut. The diamond studs in his handsome shirt caught the morning light that blazed through the bell-topped windows. He was clean shaven, the creases of his face turning into the sun darkened skin. Against it the whiteness of his hair made him appear at once older and younger. It leant a magnetism, an air of mystery to him that drew the glances of the waitresses.

Ever since his arrival they had speculated about him, about the caged vitality so plainly latent within him. He was not so obtuse as to have missed this interest, though he dismissed its implication. However, he always had a pleasant smile, a greeting, and he tipped lavishly. Any one of the three would have commanded the better than average service he received.

He ate heartily, and when he finished he wandered to the lobby and chatted with the girl at the mail desk until Dick Butler came through the wide doors.

Butler looked him over and spoke with malice. "That's a fine getup to wear prospecting. You gonna find a mine downtown here?"

Christian bestowed an indulgent smile. "Let's take a walk over to the west end of the Sandstone."

Butler was sure he was joking. Of all the mines along the reef the Sandstone had produced less paying ore than any, and the further west you went the poorer was the ground. But Christian indeed turned that way, his stride forcing Butler into a shambling trot to keep abreast.

They reached the end of pavement and followed a rutted trail that led along the lower edge of the reef, flanking the line of leases where men hurried to sink shafts into the hard rock. Continuous trains of ore wagons, of freighters hauling supplies, of men on foot made a frantic business. The word was speed and more speed as the lessees strove to raise as much ore from the deepening shafts as they could before their tenure on the ground should end.

It was no wonder, Christian had thought before, that in the disorder of these operations miners managed to steal their weight in hi-grade. There was no way to check on them, no change rooms where they could be made to strip and expose the rock they carried in their vests.

Westward along the trail the activities were less frenzied. Many holes had been started at this end of the outcropping, only to be abandoned when at twenty-five or thirty feet deep no values had been found worth carting to the mills.

Christian paused at a number of these, Butler skeptically trailing him, showing his impatience, watching his employer pick up pieces of broken rock from the dumps beside the forsaken holes.

"A man should be able to get one of these pretty cheaply," Christian said idly, and continued on as Butler grunted.

"Not too cheap. They may have stopped work, but they're hanging on on the chance a neighbor will hit the vein and boost the price of the ground."

The sun climbed the morning sky and grew hot against their backs. Butler had pulled off his coat, and sweat made large dark patches at his armpits, and at last he protested.

"How long you going to keep up this craziness?"

Christian gave him no answer, but shortly he stopped, kicked at a rock in the center of the trail and stooped for it. It was marked by wagon wheels that had rolled over it, chipped by horseshoes that had bounced it from side to side. He stood examining it, pouring over it as if it were a prize piece of hi-grade. There were ore indications, but hardly more than stains on the flinty surface. He split it by hurling it against a boulder and studied the fragments with care. Then he turned to survey the brush-covered bank above him as if to judge the direction from which the rock had fallen.

Butler moved in to peer at the piece, then snorted. "Bull quartz. You'll find tons of it on any dump in camp. I wouldn't give you five cents for the lot."

Christian looked down quizically, then abruptly dropped the pieces and began to climb the sharp slope. On his way he paused to scrape up one bit of float and then another, examining each with the intentness a jeweler would bend on a flawless diamond.

Dick Butler puffed after him in utter disgust, muttering, obviously having no faith in Christian's search.

"You've either lost your mind or you never had any to start. What do you think you're doing?"

Still Christian did not answer him, only kept climbing. He reached the edge of a raw dump, a pile of jumbled dirt and broken rock lifted and spilled from a shaft in the hillside above, and as he paused a man's tousled head appeared over the edge of the irregular hole.

The head was long, with pale blue eyes and a fair skin turned fiery red by the sun and his efforts. The man clambered out and stood above them belligerently.

"You looking for something, mister?" As he spoke he unhooked a battered bucket from the crude windless at the shaft head and stood holding it, swinging it lightly, as a weapon if one should be needed.

Christian smiled amiably. "Yes. Your lease."

The narrow head lowered, the China-blue eyes narrowed on the man below, noting the rich coat, the diamond studs, and some of the hostility in his attitude dissolved.

"Lease belongs to Schultz."

"You work for him?"

The other considered, then shrugged. "No."

"Then why are you hauling out his rock?"

Dick Butler snickered. The yellow-haired miner, a boy not over twenty, stared at the gambler with eyes as cool as Christian's, then, judging that Butler was not important here, he shifted his attention back to the

96

white-headed stranger. He used a dirt-stained hand to wipe the high arch of his narrow forehead, leaving a streak across the damp skin like an Indian's war paint.

"Schultz is lazy." He said it without rancor. "He's offered me ten percent of the lease if I find the vein. I can't get a lease of my own. You need money to get one now."

Christian, sizing him up as he talked, saw the torn shirt, the boots run over at the heels, badly cracked, the overalls washed colorless, and the thinness of the body that told him the boy had missed many meals.

He knew the type. Not for nothing had he been raised in mining camps, hunted with prospectors, listened to their yarns around their lonely camp fires. Such men did not avoid hard labor but few of them would take a salaried job. They were dreamers, independent, gambling their strength and knowledge and experience in the hardest work in the world, the battle to wrest wealth from the cracks and crevices where nature, with a suspected fiendish delight, had hidden it.

"What's your name?"

For a moment the boy hesitated, then he said, "Lars Matson." There was no real accent, but an inflection not American.

"Swedish?"

"Pa was. I was born in Central City. My mother was a Mick. You want to know anything else?"

"How'd you get to Goldfield without money?"

"Walked from Sodaville."

There was an edge to the voice. The boy did not like strangers' questions. Christian shook his head to show sympathy.

"A hot hike." He aimed a thumb at the shaft. "Find anything yet?"

He was not surprised when the boy thrust out his chin.

"What's it to you?"

"You think Schultz will sell?"

Plainly that suggestion did not please the boy, the fear showed that he might lose his chance at the percentage of the lease, yet there was a rock hard honesty in him that would not permit a direct lie.

"Maybe."

"Where can I find him?"

"In a saloon, likely. He tries one and then another." This time there was contempt in the tone.

"All right," Christian said, "go find him. Bring him to the hotel and ask for Mont Christian."

"Why should I?" Lars Matson flicked a glance at Butler, ready to fight if he were jumped.

Christian smiled again. "If he sells to me I'll give you the ten percent."

"That's what Schultz promised me."

"Yes." Christian looked at the hole in contempt. "And the way you're going you'll never make a mine. Apparently Schultz either can't or won't put up money for development and equipment. I will. Also, I'll put you on salary at a hundred dollars a month until we either strike the vein or prove to ourselves that the place is worthless."

Matson's face changed. Obviously he did not know whether this well-dressed stranger was having fun at his expense, was a foolish greenhorn, or what. He scuffed at the gravel with his worn boot toe, then finally shook his head.

"I could use that hundred, mister, but it's no go. The hole's no good, no color, no sign of the vein. I'd quit, but I got nothing else to hope on."

Christian pulled some gold pieces from his pocket and tossed them up the rise one after another. "Now you've got something."

The boy caught them and stared dazedly at the gleaming coins. "You mean it? Why?"

"To find Schultz and bring him to the hotel."

Matson looked puzzled, then shrugged and grinned. "Well, I warned you." Then he loped down the hill and turned toward town.

Butler sat on a rock, shaking his head. "You sure like throwing money around, you really do. What the ever loving hell . . . ?"

"Have you lost any on account of me?"

Butler spread his hands hopelessly.

"Then don't squeal until you're stuck." Christian turned toward the trail, leaving his henchman to follow and fret without explanation. It was not his intent to let the bully feel close to him in any degree.

Butler was still sulking an hour later when Lars Matson knocked triumphantly on Christian's door and ushered in a stocky, middle-aged man with a broad red face and small, suspicious eyes, introducing him as Adolf Schultz.

The German made no effort to shake hands. He had been drinking, but he was not drunk, curious but not enthusiastic.

"Lars says you want to buy my lease," he began in a heavy accent. "It's good ground. I make a million maybe. Lots of people getting rich."

The tone was arrogant but the eyes were defensive, and in his place beside the window Dick Butler found a butt on which to vent his mood, breaking into raucous laughter.

"Come off it, Dutchy. You haven't taken a nickel from that gopher hole and you never will."

Schultz swung on him in heavy anger. "Then what for you want to buy? Why send for me?"

Christian said sharply, "You're not doing business with Butler. I sent for you. How much do you want and how long does the lease run?"

The German swung back like a badgered bull, not understanding the situation, not wanting to let this crazy man escape yet wanting every dollar that the traffic would bear.

"She runs five months yet." He said it belligerently, then almost cringed. "I take five thousand, only because my wife is sick and I have to go by California."

"Ha," Butler jibed. "You'd take five hundred and think you'd gypped us. And you damn well would have."

Again Christian cut between them with a level voice. "Look at me, Schultz, not Butler. I won't haggle, and I never pay for a mine unless it will pay for itself. No mine operator worth the name buys unless the ore is blocked out in sight. I'll give you five hundred down and fifteen hundred more in thirty days or turn the lease back to you."

Schultz had an old country urge to bargain and began to shake his head, but Christian turned his back.

"I said I won't haggle. Show him out, Dick."

Butler heaved himself happily from his chair. "A pleasure. Come on, Dutchy, vamoose now." He grabbed Schultz' arm and was propelling him toward the door.

Schultz was forced into a running step until he reached the panel, and there he caught a firm grip on the knob and hung on, digging in his feet, twisting to look back at Christian.

"You pay me fifteen hundred in thirty days?"

Christian said carelessly, "Or turn the lease back. You'll gain at least by having your shaft deepened at no cost."

"I take it. I take it." The man clung to the door, bobbing his torso with the eagerness of the fright at having so nearly lost what he believed was far the best of the bargain.

Christian was pleased. He hoped that in thirty days the mine would have served its purpose, when he would gladly return the barren hole to Schultz.

Butler had stepped away and stood grinning heavily at the spectacle of the German, who threw him a glance and then trotted back to Christian.

"You pay now."

Christian dropped five hundred in twenties on the table at his side, saying, "Where's the paper that says you hold the lease?"

"Paper?" Schultz' face went blank. "I've got no paper."

"Then how do I know you've got the right to sell?"

The man waved his hands. "Mr. Pierson will tell you."

Alfred Pierson, Christian had learned, headed the syndicate that controlled the Sandstone, and had an office on Fremont Street. Christian scooped up the gold and dropped it into his pocket while Schultz watched hungrily. Then they all filed from the room, Lars Matson, silent, watching Dick Butler with open scorn as Christian locked his door.

Although the upper end of the Sandstone claim had already produced some hundred thousand dollars, the company offices were not impressive. There was a small private office behind a single room which held a roll-top desk, an iron safe, a flat table at which two clerks worked, and four straight-backed chairs.

Mr. Pierson was not present, but a clerk volunteered the information that at this hour he could usually be found at the Northern, and Butler was sent to locate him. They returned shortly, Pierson a bustling little man with heavy glasses and a birdlike manner.

"I've noticed you around," he greeted Christian affably. "Dick tells me you want to buy Schultz' lease."

"If he has one." Christian sounded skeptical.

"Oh, he has it all right, although if I'd realized what a lazy clod he is he would never have been given it." The company man threw the German a scathing glance.

"He has no paper to prove it?"

102

Pierson looked surprised, then he laughed lightly, pattered to the safe and dragged out a dog-eared note book, opened it on the table and scanned a page with his bird-claw finger.

Christian, reading across the small shoulder, saw the Spencerian script at the head of the page, *Schultz Lease* and read below, the description of the property and the date of expiration of the contract. The agreement specified that forty percent of the returns from the mine be paid to the Sandstone Company. That was all that was written on the page. The simplicity struck Christian as curious. He knew that one lease on the Mohawk alone had produced five million.

"Is this the normal kind of agreement here?"

Pierson's eyes twinkled with amusement. "I know you haven't been in Goldfield long, sir, but this is how we do things here. It's all come about so rapidly, you know. Jim Butler and Tasker Oddie began the system when they made the original discovery and those of us who have followed have had no time nor reason to change. Believe me, any of these lease agreements will stand up in court. They have already been tested several times."

"And how is it signified if I buy Schultz' lease?"

"I simply enter the terms on this page. If you make the final payment the lease will be yours to work for the next five months, and may you be as lucky as some have."

"All right," said Christian. "When in Rome . . ." He again took out the money and paid it over to the

German, saw the transaction entered, and then led Butler and Lars Matson back to the street.

Butler mocked him. "So that's your way of finding a mine, after all the good prospects I herded in to you. You're some mining genius, all right."

"You talk too much, Dick. And you're not paid to think."

Christian's face was inscrutable. "Listen to me now, and do as I say. Go down to one of the butcher shops and get me a green bull hide, the greener the better. If they butchered it this morning, that's fine."

Dick Butler's truculence came up and he stood, head down, refusal to obey moving on his loose lips.

"Also, get one of those new tin washtubs I saw in front of the hardware store."

Butler's mouth opened as it seemed to him that he was being ridiculed, then it closed at the glint in Christian's eye, and he turned stolidly away on the errand.

Christian did not watch after him but looked at once at the yellow-haired boy.

"You have dynamite at the shaft?"

"Not yet. I didn't have the price."

Christian handed him coins. "Get a box and meet me at the lease an hour from now." For himself, he swung toward the newspaper office.

Lars Matson was there, sitting on the case of powder, and Butler, keeping his distance from the bull skin that was already beginning to stink beneath a blanket of flies, when Christian led two men from the Goldfield News and half a dozen curious trailers up the bank.

Ignoring the shaft, he angled off to the right along the ridge, bending to study the ground until he chose a spot. There he stopped and called to Matson to bring a single jack and sledge, and with a broken branch drew a small pattern in the rocky soil, an area that could be wholly covered by the reeking hide.

"Drill me five holes inside there," he said, and stepped back.

Lars looked at him doubtfully, looked at the faint outcrop of quartz that showed through the dust, and shrugged. It was obvious that he shared Dick Butler's doubts about Christian's common sense. But he had been paid, and he would work for the money. Underfleshed as he was, he was still strong and he sank the drill steadily, cleaning the holes with care as he went.

The newspapermen climbed to watch, to judge the promise of the site for themselves. Don Davis chewed on an aromatic twig, his eyes sardonic.

"That don't look like bonanza to me. What gives you the idea you'll find anything there?"

Christian showed no concern, settling comfortably onto a rock, crossing his knees. "I bet you fifty dollars, didn't I?"

Davis glanced at his partner and winked. A snigger ran through the little audience, but the gambling spirit that marked the camp held them through the wait in the summer sunshine.

Lars paused to pull off his ragged shirt, spat on his palms and again lifted the heavy sledge. Sweat shone on his back but he worked rhythmically through one hole, two, three. On the fourth his aim faltered as he tired.

Christian got up from his rock and deliberately unbuttoned his coat, shucked out of it, folded it and thrust it offhandedly at Davis. He removed the dress vest and then the starched shirt and passed them to the reporter. Then, in his elegant trousers and shoes designed for city streets, he stepped to Matson and waved him away.

He made an incongruous figure, lifting the mall, hefting its five-pound weight tentatively, but he appeared not to notice. He examined the drill, already dulled by the rock. He would have preferred to sharpen it, but that would take time, during which he might lose his gallery.

It was many years since he had drilled a hole and his muscles, unaccustomed to this particular use, began to protest before he had driven the drill two feet into the rotten quartz, yet he worked on, waiting for the second wind, for the adjustment of the tendons hardened by prison labor.

Sweat ran into his eyes, mingling with the acrid dust that rose in little puffs from the hole with each strike of the hammer, each twist of the drill. He stopped once to ease his back and then drove on, and at length bottomed out the plug at five feet. He cleaned it, used a linen handkerchief to wipe the mud from his face, then straightened and called to Lars to bring the powder box.

The boy carried it forward, his face without expression, lowered the box to the ground and knocked off the lid. As he reached inside Christian waved him away and lifted out three sticks for each hole. Matson uttered a wordless protest that he was overloading the shots and then, looking around at the attending group, fell well out of range.

Christian too looked about him and the men, taking the cue, followed the boy to a safe distance. They watched, passing their judgments, and Christian broke the sticks, squeezed out the doughy mixture and moulded five single rolls, each just under two inches in diameter so that they could be forced into the holes. What they could not see as he knelt over the bores was that from the belt beneath his trousers band he freed the small pouch of gold dust.

As he tamped down the dynamite he spilled in about two ounces of gold. Then he set the caps, crimped them to the fuse and strung this across the rocks, down beneath the edge of the reef.

Now he beckoned Butler in with the bull hide and stretched it over the charged area, weighting its edges with stones as heavy as he could find.

Don Davis called, laughing. "That'll never hold her down."

Christian seemed not to hear, to be a man wholly concentrating on the job he was doing. That finished, he returned to the far end of the fuse, cast a look about to be sure everyone was safely below the reef, lighted the fuse and jumped for cover.

Huddled in the shadow of the bare rock he counted, but the seconds dragged. It seemed an interminable time before the charges went off. Then with a giant roar, as if the animal had come to furious life, the bull hide arched high into the air, creating a tent that caught most of the loose rock, kept it from scattering as it was propelled upward.

Some chunks did fly from under it and rained down about the men crouched against the rock shelter. One small sliver nicked Butler's cheek, but no one else was hit.

As the noise and dust subsided the group rose and moved intently to where the seared hide had fallen, close to the lip of the freshly blasted pit. Christian was in the lead, calling back to Lars to bring the washtub. Butler leant a hand and the two of them half filled the vessel with water from the barrel beside the old shaft, then hauled it to the new pit.

Christian, handling the hide gently, rinsed it with care, washing out all of the fine dust driven into the skin by the force of the blast. When he was satisfied, the bottom of the tub held a layer of powdered sand. While he let this settle he reclaimed his coat from Davis, got the flour sack from the pocket and handed it to Lars. He spilled away most of the water in the tub, stirred the remainder into roiling, and poured this through the sack. Finally, he dropped the sack into the gold pan that Lars had been using to wash his samples and set it afire. In this process any sand caught in the cloth would be freed.

Without being told, Lars and Butler had brought another tub of water, and as the crowd gathered in close, Christian lowered the pan into the tub and began to wash the sand around with the swinging, swirling motion.

No one had spoken since the blast, although the audience had been augmented by miners drawn from nearby workings by the unprecedented power of the shot. All were intent on the slowly turning pan, on what could be seen at its bottom as the lighter ash and sand were flushed out, over its rim.

Gradually the darker sand was cleaned and moved sluggishly in a shifting fan beneath the water. Tiny flakes of yellow appeared and multiplied along the fan's trailing edge. A solid rim of the precious dust developed.

Lars Matson, crouched at Christian's side, drew breath deeply, raggedly, into his hollow chest, and then gave out a warwhoop. He leaped upright, jumping up and down.

"We got a mine. We got a mine. We got a mine."

Dick Butler spoke in a stunned, hoarse whisper. "Must be three ounces in that pan. Maybe four."

Christian, without rising, silently extended the pan to Don Davis. The newspaperman looked into it, his lips twisting in reluctant recognition.

"If I hadn't watched it I wouldn't believe it. Mister, I guess I owe you fifty dollars."

Mont Christian stood up, finding it easy to summon the smile he wanted.

"Forget it. If this mine is as rich as I think I won't need your money. I just wanted to prove a point."

He was eminently pleased. He had accomplished his purpose. He had assured himself publicity, had established Mont Christian in Goldfield's mind as a man to be given heed to.

CHAPTER
ELEVEN

He was not wrong. All mining-town newspapers love a local story of unexpected wealth to advertise their camp, and the *News* was no exception. With a banner head they blazoned the word that Mont Christian, late of Mexico, had found a rich new lead on his Sandstone lease. They could not say enough for the discovery, estimating that the ore might rival that of the Mohawk, which had been averaging out at better than thirty-five hundred dollars to the ton.

In any other camp the news would have been staggering, but in Goldfield superlatives were commonplace, and the citizens accepted it without question, without hurrah.

Still, it attracted the attention Christian wanted. He had named the shaft the "Emma" and it was so carried in the paper, and Amos Frost, who missed little that went on around him, picked up the meaning at once.

Home for supper on the evening after Christian's staged explosion, he sat at the end of the table with the girl facing him, the two children between them. Relishing this new chance for cruelty, he ate his steak slowly, sat back with his coffee and the small glass of cherry brandy, and not until then mentioned the story. As if it were an afterthought he drew the folded paper from his pocket, waggled it and said to the girl;

"I see your man hit it rich yesterday."

Emma Bondford had been sitting silent, her eyes on her plate, feeling that her taut drawn nerves must surely soon snap. This was the third evening since she had so determinedly walked out of the house and then forced herself to return, yet Frost had made not one reference to the subject, not, she knew, that he would overlook it, but that he was merely biding his time.

Now she started, making no sense of his caustic words. "What did you say?"

Again he flourished the paper, passing it down the table. "Read for yourself. Your man looks to get rich, if you can believe the *News*. I told you you should have grabbed him off."

She read slowly, her puzzlement growing. Glad for Mont Christian, there was something about the story that bothered her.

"Why did he do it that way? It sounds as if he were purposely trying to attract attention."

Amos Frost had arrived at the same conclusion, and Christian's intention had him guessing. He wanted to think about it, but now the children were making a hullabaloo about their friend's new wealth and the chances that he would buy them a pony, demanding to be taken to see him at once.

"Not tonight," he said shortly, picked up the *News* and went for his hat.

Emma Bondford would have liked to read the article again, but she was too relieved that he was leaving the house to risk asking to keep the paper.

Pie Berman was sitting at one of the small tables at the rear of the saloon, across from Sally Ringe, when Frost came up, saying without preamble;

"Get lost."

The bouncer rose without sign of resentment, and Frost dropped into the vacated chair.

"You've seen the Christian story? What do you make of it?"

Sally shrugged. "Looks like Goldfield has a new mine."

"What else?"

"Either the man's a fool or he's playing some game. Maybe he bought a lot of Sandstone stock and figures that this trick will send the price jumping tomorrow and he can sell out fat."

"I thought that might be it. Send someone to fetch Thomas and Hickman. And Farrel. Let's find out."

When the messenger was gone, Sally turned back, chuckling. "This kind of answers your idea that he's a Pinkerton agent, doesn't it?"

But Frost was not in a mood to laugh. "Does it? Suppose he thought I was getting suspicious, wouldn't he likely pull a stunt such as this to throw me off guard?"

"Well, maybe," the woman admitted. "Then you really believe he is?"

"A Pinkerton man went to see him at the hotel."

Still Sally Ringe shook her head. "I can smell a policeman a mile away, and from what I've seen this joker doesn't fill the bill. He's up to something, I agree, but my guess would be that it's a fancy stock swindle."

Frost's eyes glittered. "If it's that, he'll find us sitting right on his shoulder."

Twenty minutes later the group gathered in the rear room, listened to Frost's suspicion about the story, and put their minds on the problem.

"Was there any unusual activity in Sandstone stock this last week or so?"

Weldon Thomas, the broker, shook his head. "It's still steady at about sixty cents."

"How many shares are outstanding?"

"Maybe a million."

"Who holds control?"

"That's hard to say. Al Pierson is still president, but I think he unloaded most of his holding months ago. I can tell you in the morning when I look at the stock book."

"What did their promotion stock close at?"

"Forty cents."

"Then there hasn't been a lot of buying."

"Not yet," said Thomas, "but there's bound to be some activity after this publicity. I'd say it would probably open ten to fifteen cents up in the morning."

Frost moistened his already damp lips. "I wonder if he really found anything."

They brooded with him, all thinking along the same lines and Frost putting their worries into words.

"There's something very fishy about Mr. Mont Christian. We haven't laid a finger on one minute of his past history, and no man alive can live that long without leaving some kind of print. There's no record of a bank deposit in any bank here or in San Francisco, which means he has no credit on the coast, yet from the gossip he's a rich mining man. What's he doing, carrying a fortune around in a sack?"

They chuckled without humor.

"I still think he's a Pinkerton. I think his little show this afternoon was meant as a red herring to convince us he's really looking for a gold mine."

"So let's get rid of him." James Farrel believed in direct action. He had not the wit for subtlety.

Amos Frost was tempted, but still held off. "Sally already suggested that, but not yet. Let's see what he does tomorrow, find out if he's bought heavily in Sandstone. He's made his move; let's just lie low and watch awhile."

Everybody else in Goldfield was suddenly watching Mont Christian. Overnight he had become another celebrity in the camp. Men who had apparently not noticed him before went out of their way to speak to him on the street. It was no secret when Al Pierson sent a messenger who found Christian at breakfast and escorted him back to the Sandstone office.

The little president squinted at him across the desk neither friendly nor unfriendly. "That was quite a stunt you put on yesterday afternoon. I thought every dodge that could draw publicity had already been pulled in Goldfield, but you topped them."

Christian's grin was relaxed, and Pierson leaned forward, lowering his voice.

"So do you mind if I ask you what you're up to? Naturally I'm interested, since your lease is on our ground."

Mont Christian had spent some of his waiting period thoroughly investigating the Sandstone company along with other companies, and he had chosen Sandstone because it appeared to be ripe for his uses. The concern had been incorporated only the year before, buying out seventeen hundred feet of claims on the western end of the reef from the Hoffa brothers.

It had been a promotion deal from the first. Pierson and his associates had paid the Hoffas five thousand in money, which the brothers lost over the tables at the Northern in twenty minutes. The remaining price, fifty thousand shares of stock at fifty cents a share, Ham and Sam Hoffa sold at once and ran through the proceeds. At last reports they were prospecting around the Beatty district on the edge of Death Valley.

The Sandstone syndicate, lacking development capital, divided the ground into seventeen parcels and assigned each for a six-month period.

It was one of these leases that Christian had acquired from Schultz, toward the extreme west end where the values were proving negligible. The only reason Sandstone stock hung near its original price was that the three eastern parcels had produced close to a hundred thousand dollars worth of ore.

By Goldfield standards this was chicken feed, but it had enabled the parent company to declare a ten-cent dividend.

116

Christian was casual. "I'll make a trade with you. I'll give you day-by-day mill reports on what we dig if you'll give me a list of your larger stockholders."

Pierson thought this over. "You meaning to buy in?"

No, Christian thought, he did not intend buying into this company. He meant to continue salting the ore he pulled from his shaft, salt it heavily enough to attract notice, to drive the stock higher than it had any right to be. That, he felt sure, would bring Amos Frost and his group around, looking for a profit. If he could get them to make a heavy investment, then he would quit pouring his dust into the barren hole, and when the rock showed no values the stock would plummet. But first he had to know if any of that group were already holding any sizable amount of Sandstone stock. He gave Pierson a twisting smile.

"Are you in control?"

Pierson flushed. He had, Christian knew, done what many mine owners had done before him, sold most of his stock to the unsuspecting public, pocketed the money, and retained only shares enough to keep him in the presidency which paid him a salary of five thousand a year.

"I've sold some," he admitted reluctantly.

Christian winked at him. Prison had made him cynical. He knew that Pierson would rob him if he could and had no scruples in hoodwinking the company man.

"What about a mill — does Sandstone own one?"

"We have an interest in a ten-stamp setup at the east end of our holdings. That is, it's owned by a few of us as individuals, not by the company."

That too was common practice. A syndicate's officers banded together to build a mill, then funneled all ore from their property through it, charging the leasers high prices for treating what they produced and diverting the mill profits from the company treasury into their own pockets.

"That's all right with me," Christian nodded equably, "It will be about a week before we're ready to start hauling ore." He did not care that Pierson's expression said he took this man for a fool or a dreamer or both. "Now, the stock list."

Pierson summoned a clerk and directed him to copy the list and the amount of stock held in each name, and send it over to Christian's hotel. Mont left the office, satisfied with the progress of his plan.

He walked across town toward his mine, thinking that now he would have to have a horse and buggy, a status symbol in this camp, indicating his importance.

At the lease he found that Lars Matson had, according to his orders, already hired six men, and all were busy. Two worked in the shallow shaft, drilling for shots that would sink the hole deeper. Lars and the others had hauled in two loads of rough lumber and were building a headframe, a tool house, bunk house, and cook shack. Watching their labor, Christian was tempted. He threw off his dress coat and went to work, helping at the headframe to hang the pulleys that would raise the loaded ore buckets.

After his long inaction it was good to work with his hands again, and he knew a passing regret that what they were doing was merely for show, that the hole they were punching into the rotten reef would never make a mine.

He had known the fascination of digging into the earth in search of metal. Mining was in his blood, as it had been in his father's, and nothing in the world could match for him the thrill of making a real strike. But he put away his rise of feeling and settled coldly to his purpose.

The hole was still so shallow that the powder fumes from each blast cleared quickly. They drilled, shot, mucked out the broken rock and drilled again. They alternated crews with each shot, so that two thirds of the time each man worked above ground. Christian saw that the miners were experienced, and his opinion of Lars Matson grew as the day progressed. The boy worked without lagging, with no wasted motion.

Dick Butler arrived and Christian sent him back to town to rent a team and light wagon, and they kept him shuttling back and forth, fetching supplies as their need was anticipated.

At noon, while the miners ate in the shade of the rising tool house, Christian beckoned Matson and they walked out through the brush, looking for the small stone pyramids that marked the corners of the lease. It ran a hundred feet along the reef and back eight hundred from the rock upthrust that was the outcropping of ore.

When they had moved out of earshot Christian said, "That's a good crew you've got. I'm surprised you were lucky enough to get them, considering how busy the mines are."

Matson gave him a tight grin. "After what you turned up yesterday half the men in camp would jump at the chance. They figure you've got luck, that another fifty feet will put us in hi-grade, and they can start grabbing."

Christian's smile was chill as he pictured the disappointment they had coming. He did not mean to salt the rock while they could steal it. He would not add the gold until the ore was in the carts, on the way to the mill.

But the men were eager. No shaft ever went down faster. They averaged ten feet a day, with the rock's character changing as they drove deeper into the earth, in some spots being so rotten that the drills almost sank of their own weight.

Christian paid little attention to the hole. His only interest lay in getting down a hundred feet, so that when the ore began to show values they would not be suspected on the basis of surface indications. Thus, he was wholly unprepared for the surprise he was dealt at the end of the sixth day.

The buildings were finished, the ore buckets lifted and dropped on the windlass. The shaft was designed wide enough to accommodate a two-compartment hoist, for Christian meant to bring up a steam engine when the work was deep enough. Meantime, length after length of ladder was being put down for the men's use, and now descended sixty feet.

They had had a small audience since morning, people squatting on the hillside watching the progress, for word had run along the reef that the shaft was being sunk in record time.

At five o'clock the earth-stained miners climbed to the surface and headed toward town. Dick Butler took the rented team to the livery stable, and Lars Matson went down the ladders with dynamite to blow the last shot of the day, to have a load ready for raising in the morning. It was the signal for the audience to drift away. By the time Lars came up to set off the blast he and Christian were alone.

Mont watched him return as the fumes cleared, a careful workman checking his job. The lamp on his cap was a pinpoint seen from ground level, but at the bottom it pushed back the shadows in the rough pit. Mont waited, not wanting to leave any man down there, in case of trouble, sitting idly at the rude table in the cubicle office beside the headframe.

"Mr. Christian! Mr. Christian!"

The shout sounded like a muffled shriek, rising from the depths. Christian leaped up and ran to the shaft. All kinds of accidents could happen in a mine. The blast might have torn a section of ladder loose and dropped Matson in a bone crushing fall. He peered over the stone curbing that protected the lip of the hole and far below saw the wink of light.

"What is it? You hurt?"

The boy's voice had an ominously choked sound. "Come on down here."

Christian swung over the edge, his feet feeling for the rungs of the vertical ladder, and scrambled down with the speed of acquired skill. Without his lamp he could see nothing, he would have to trust to Matson's light to learn what had happened, and again he called.

"Are you hurt?"

"No." The voice was still tight. "Want you to see something."

Relief let Christian's irritation rise. If that was all, the boy could have told him and saved him the descent. He dropped on down the ladder carelessly until his feet struck the loose rock of the bottom and stepped into the radiance of Matson's lamp. It cast its glow against the place where the blast had cut away a portion of the wall, and Lars was on his knees, staring at this spot.

"Look. Look at this."

Christian bent over his shoulder. They had begun by following the vein down, but it had tipped to the west and they had continued straight, mainly through county rock. The last blast had kicked out a chunk of the foot wall as large as a calf and it lay in one piece at the far side of the area. Where it had been a patch of the quartz stringer hung exposed.

In his irritation Christian said, "What about it? We knew the vein was pitching." Then he cut his words short.

The quartz was not the same color as the dyke they had followed from the surface. This had a blue cast like a batik in indigo. Seeing the darker threads, Christian moved closer, feeling the pulse of excitement throb against his throat. There could be no doubt. Lacing through the tiny fissures were stringers of gold. Wire gold. Pure, free milling gold.

To prove that his eyes were not tricking him he opened his long-bladed knife and pried out one long, thick hair. Jarred loose by the explosion, a two-inch section came free.

He cradled it in the palm of his hand, feeling its weight. Above the rush of his thoughts he heard Matson's frenzied babbling.

"We've hit it. We've hit the true vein. It's the same as in the Mohawk ground. I've seen it, and some of that runs thirty-five hundred to the ton."

Christian did not answer, and the boy took his silence for doubt.

"I tell you. I'd know that blue formation anywhere. It's a different lead from the one up top. Mohawk struck it at ten feet, but it must dip down. All the ground between here and the Red Top must carry it. They haven't gone deep enough. Mr. Christian, we've got a mine, a great mine. And we've still got near five months on the lease. We're rich."

Abruptly Mont Christian began to laugh, with an uncontrollable convulsion of sound that ricocheted from wall to wall. He had meant to salt this hole, to create an illusion of a honey pot of wealth that would draw Amos Frost's gold-hungry swarm into a move by which he could trap them. He had not cared whether they chose to invest in the rising Sandstone stock and lose when he revealed the true barrenness of the ground, or whether they attempted to euchre him out of the lease, and put themselves into a position in which he could expose them.

Now that device was impossible. The hole was mocking him. His false mine had become real, and there was no way to foretell how rich it was, but surely the small block of stock Frost already held could only add to his fortune.

Mont Christian had what every man in Goldfield dreamed of finding, and sheer accident had brought it to him. No one else would have dug so far without a trace of promising color. No one else would have selected a spot at random, started directly down and continued straight when what vein there was angled away.

The irony shook him. His laughter was at himself and at the struggle of man to control his own fate. If Schultz had kept the lease he and Matson would have quit in disgust long before they reached this level. If this last blast had not knocked out the section of side wall they could have dug on, parallel to the true vein and never known it. All of this burned through his mind as he stared at the glowing trifle in his hand and knew that he must make another plan. Then he composed his face and looked at the boy.

"Well, let's see what we have. Get the drill and singlejack and let's blow out that wall. Watch yourself," he added as Matson slipped and stumbled in his haste. "Now isn't the time for you to fall off that ladder."

Matson giggled foolishly in his fever. He had already put in twelve hours that day, but such was his eagerness for gold that he worked as if he were freshly rested.

They took turns, one with the sledge, one twisting the drill. They punched six holes, three at the top of the drift they were starting, three at the bottom. Then they climbed to the surface, reeling out the fuse. The sound of the shot was dulled by the depth at which it exploded, and before the echoes died Christian looked at the boy.

"Go find Dick Butler, tell him to get a heavier wagon and a team, and bring half-a-dozen barrels."

Matson gaped, puzzled, and Christian's tone sharpened. "Go on. Move. And both of you keep your mouths shut."

He listened as the boy's running footsteps died. The sun was near the rim of the western hills, and the day was still hot. From the east along the reef, noise reached him from those mines already proven valuable, where shifts were kept busy around the clock. But nothing moved within half a mile of where he stood. This portion of the ridge was deserted at this hour.

He waited until the powder fumes cleared sufficiently, then took a cap with a light and went down the ladder.

The sight at the bottom he would never forget. The dynamite had opened a six-foot high, five-foot wide gap in the wall. When he had cleared away the rubble, using a pick to pry pieces as big as his body into the shaft, he found himself in a rough cave, with the blue quartz all around him. The filigree of gold stringers lacing through it took his breath. Never, in the camps he had visited with his father as a boy, or while he mined on his own before the prison had closed on him, had he seen anything to approach this.

He had heard stories of the richness of the Mohawk but had discounted them as exaggeration; yet he knew that the shattered rock at his feet would easily run four thousand dollars to the ton. It was unheard of. And his mind flashed to the knowledge that the ore body might well extend from the Mohawk, clear through the Red Top and the full length of the Sandstone ground. Yet none of these neighbors had found it, they had not driven deep enough, or where they had, they had been on one side or the other, and unless they cross-cut they must miss it as he had nearly done.

Cold, dedicated to revenge as he had become, he was shaken by the rush of a born miner's elation. Yet he choked it off. Tempted to fill his pockets with all the ore he could carry, he chose instead several small pieces that showed exceptional value, and with them slowly climbed the ladder.

When at dusk the wagon approached, the jingle of the harness running before it, Mont Christian was again the withdrawn creature that so puzzled those who knew him. He watched Dick Butler rein in, noted Lars Matson on the high seat at his side, saw the wagon bed filled with empty barrels, and said only,

"We've got a night's work ahead of us."

Butler cursed openly. "What do you mean?"

"There's a spring half a mile west of here, I've heard."

"I know where it is," Matson nodded. "But the water's not good for much, too alkali."

126

"It will do for our need." Christian tossed three ore buckets into the wagon and swung up to Matson's side. "Drive down to the spring, Dick. You've been complaining that you hadn't enough to do. You're going to earn your money tonight."

They did not comprehend, and he did not explain. Mont Christian kept his reputation for being close mouthed.

CHAPTER
TWELVE

In the morning Mont Christian found that Lars Matson had, among his other abilities, a flair for acting.

When the miners gathered for the day's work Lars, according to his custom, was first down the shaft, to check the conditions before he sent his men below. But he returned up the ladder immediately, his face long with consternation, saying in a gloomy tone,

"We won't be drilling down there today."

Christian, examining the bit of a drill, lifted his head sharply. "Why not?"

"Water." The word was a curse.

Disbelief ran through the men. Petrie, built like an ape, lifted a long arm to scratch his head and spat.

"Aw, I never worked in a drier hole. We ain't had more than a trickle all the way down."

"We've got more now," Matson was dolorous. "Maybe that wind-up shot last night busted into a seam."

As he spoke he picked up a piece of broken rock from the growing dump and tossed it over the low wall. Fifty feet below the splash echoed upward. Petrie's mouth dropped open and with the others he went to peer into the shaft. Then with one accord they looked at Christian.

Mont appeared to hesitate as if confused by this development, then he too picked up a rock and shouldered in, dropping it into the dark void. Seconds later the sound came back, unmistakable. A low sigh from the miners answered it. Water, indeed. Water had ruined more mines than any other factor. It had drowned the great bonanza of Virginia City. It had stopped the work at a frustratingly shallow level in Tombstone. Sometimes it could be held back by pumps, but there were also inexhaustable underground rivers that no pumps could handle.

Christian did not look at the watching circle of faces. He reached for a lamp, fastened it to his hat and stepped onto the ladder. What he found at the bottom was the seven feet of spring water that he, Matson and Butler had laboriously hauled and dumped into the hole. It had taken most of the night, but it did effectively conceal all sign of the hi-grade that had been uncovered.

He climbed back with reluctant slowness, saying nothing, taking his time removing the lamp and returning it to its place.

Matson said tensely, "What do you think?"

Christian lifted his shoulders and dropped them. "I'd say ten or twelve feet. We won't work today. Maybe we won't ever work this hole again."

The miners exchanged quick glances. One said tentatively;

"The Mohawk's got an extra pump. They put a new one in last month and . . ."

"And pumps cost money," Christian finished the sentence. "I'll have to see what I can do. That hole has cost me already, and the color hasn't held up."

To that last they could all testify, and the men who had been so eager to sign on with "Lucky" Christian had begun to wonder, to doubt his luck and question his sanity in continuing the unpromising probe. But that was mining. They shrugged off their hopes of filling their hi-grade vests at this man's expense and followed him to the office shack.

Christian paid them off in silence and watched them move down the trail toward town. Within an hour, he knew, the word that the Emma had flooded would be the topic of conversation in every bar in Goldfield.

After his stunt with the bull hide, Sandstone stock had risen until it closed the night before at seventy cents a share. It would plummet now. Even though its eastern leases were producing, the threat of water would spread its suspicion to them, and the mercurial favor of those who dealt in mines would vanish.

That was what Christian wanted. However he employed the Emma, he must now acquire full control of Sandstone, and all of his Mexican gold could not buy that at seventy cents a share. Thus he had set the stage to bring the price within his reach.

Now he called Lars Matson and Dick Butler to him.

"I told you I'd make money for you," he said, "but you'll have to play a careful part now, and follow my orders. I will put up five thousand dollars for each of you, to buy stock, but you must neither buy until I tell you to nor sell without my leave. And Dick, if you so much as touch a bottle of whiskey from now on I'll break your worthless neck. Do you both agree?"

"Don't worry." Butler was already caught up in his dream. Lars Matson's eyes held a dogged devotion.

"Then," said Christian, "let us go to town. Dick, you spend the day in one of the brokerage houses. Your mine is flooded and worthless, so look it, believe it. Watch the board and when it closes come and tell me what Sandstone did."

"Lars, go see how cheaply you can buy that Mohawk pump, and what's wrong with it. Tonight the three of us will dine at the Palm Grill, a sour, dejected party trying to put the best face on a dismal failure."

Butler's report at that dinner was that Sandstone had spun dizzily down to a closing price below thirty, with whole blocks offered at twenty-five that found no takers.

In the morning it opened at twenty and continued to slide. The rush was on to unload Sandstone. Mont Christian made his way to Al Pierson's office and unobtrusively set the heavy satchel he carried on the floor beside his chair. Pierson's greeting was bleak, and he fidgeted nervously.

"Water." He repeated it over and over, and Christian waited, letting him pour out his misery. "And I'm still sitting on a trunk full of the stock."

Sixty thousand shares, Christian knew, which he intended to buy with the gold in the satchel. But first he wanted to be sure Pierson would sell at his first offer, he wanted no haggling.

"Maybe it isn't too bad," he said. "Your other leases are still dry, aren't they?"

"They aren't as deep as you are."

The man was thoroughly disconsolate, and then he surprised Christian and played right into his hand.

"The trouble is, just last week I borrowed twelve thousand from the bank to go into a deal in Tonopah, and they just sent a message that they need more collateral. You haven't got twelve thousand you'd loan me, have you?" He said this last as an afterthought, not as if he had any real hope.

"No," Christian shook his head slowly, "but I might buy your Sandstone for twelve. I still believe in the ground, and I think I can lick the water. That would figure twenty cents, above the present market price."

"All of it?" Pierson was taken aback by Christian's promptness, and caution touched him. "Say fifty thousand shares for twelve. Let me keep ten, let me stay inside."

Christian's lips twisted. "And stay president, is that it?"

The man squirmed.

"All right, it's a deal. Meet me at the bank in half an hour."

Mont Christian rose unhurriedly and left the office, going directly to George Nixon's bank. As he was ushered in to the president Nixon rose and offered his hand. Christian took it, saying,

"I'm Mont Christian . . ."

"I know who you are." Nixon's tight-lipped mouth smiled a trifle but his eyes did not relax their gimlet gaze. "I think everyone in town knows you. I understand you're having a little water trouble?"

His manner told that he feared the white-haired celebrity would ask for a loan, which he had no intention of making. Instead, Christian lifted the heavy satchel and set it on the desk.

"This is gold dust from Mexico," he said. "More than enough to pay off Al Pierson's loan. I'm buying some of his Sandstone stock."

George Nixon was known as one of the coolest gamblers and best businessmen in Goldfield. He showed no trace of surprise as Christian opened the bag, displaying the dust. He said only,

"You're carrying that around town pretty carelessly. You have any more?"

"About fifty thousand worth, I don't know exactly. I had to leave Sonora fast. The Indians killed my partner and nearly finished me."

The banker did not question this. Things were so unsettled below the line that anything could happen in the rough mountains of northern Mexico.

"I think you'd be safer," he said, "by turning it in to us for credit."

"Perhaps you're right. I'll bring it in today." Mont did not explain why he had not done so before. But he had wanted to establish an identity as a local mining man first. Nixon would not today question his possession of the gold as he might have when Mont first arrived in town.

He stood casually as Nixon touched a bell and directed the clerk who answered to bring a gold scale, while the twelve thousand was weighed out and the transaction completed, and was wryly amused that the banker's curiosity took another direction.

"Apparently the water at the Emma doesn't trouble you?"

Christian shrugged. "I'm a gambler. I think pumps will handle it."

"And you still have faith in the shaft?"

Christian repeated his shrug. "Gold is where you find it. I can't effectively buy into the Mohawk or the Red Top or their like, and my luck has been good before."

When Pierson had arrived, when the stock was transferred into his name, Christian left the bank owning his first large block of Sandstone stock. He located Lars Matson and with his new light rig moved his two gold laden boxes from the hotel to the bank, where Nixon gave him a receipt for fifty-two thousand dollars on deposit.

But he was not yet content with the day. He must find more Sandstone stock. He wanted as many of the million outstanding shares as he could get. But even at twenty cents he could not buy full control and retain enough of his capital to develop the lease, for although hi-grade was in sight it would take time and work to deepen the shaft, to open cross-cuts into the vein and put in proper hoisting equipment.

And he knew that he had tipped his hand to George Nixon. He would have to move fast now. Standing on the street outside the bank he stopped to think. Perhaps he should have told the banker about the find, enlisted his help in securing control. Nixon and his partner Winfield were the most important men in camp; they already controlled the Mohawk, and rumor said their holdings in the Red Top were extensive.

He was on the point of turning back into the bank when a startling realization struck him. In the excitement of the last few hours he had not once thought of Amos Frost. He was behaving like a man only interested in his own fortune. He had forgotten his purpose for being in Goldfield.

And with that realization his purpose hardened. Also, he knew how to accomplish his end. He would not buy full control of Sandstone. He would lure his enemies into buying, and acquire for himself only enough that their joint holdings would be the controlling block. He would win their confidence by making riches for them, and then lead them to their destruction.

He swung away, down Goxel, toward the offices of Weldon Thomas and Company, brokers.

Coming into the crowded customers' room he paused to read the latest quotations, which two hurrying boys were chalking on the big blackboard. He watched a sale of a thousand shares of Sandstone at eighteen recorded, another two thousand at fifteen.

Then a bell rang, signaling that the exchange was closing for the day. Men rose from the long benches and gathered into groups to discuss the action of the board. Christian detoured around them, down the depth of the big room to the cashier's cage at the rear. He stopped before the grilled window and looked through into the well where two dozen clerks labored to record the day's trades on their customer reports. The cashier, a tall man with a bald dome of a head and a beaked nose, came forward.

"Help you?"

"I want to talk to Mr. Thomas."

The cashier hesitated. "We're pretty busy right now . . ."

"I know, with the market just closing. It's about the market that I want to see him."

In Goldfield a broker did not refuse to see anyone. The dirtstained miner in work clothes might have a quarter of a million to invest in stock, and Mont Christian looked very prosperous. The clerk bowed.

"What name?"

His eyes flicked at the answer, and he turned away to the corner office. Moments later Weldon Thomas came out to greet Christian.

This was one of the group that had stolen his Tombstone mine and railroaded him to Yuma prison, yet there was no sign of recognition, no hint of memory in the face, only a wariness as to what the visit meant. Thomas had run to fat. Christian would not have known him as the lean, half-starved prospector who had roamed the Arizona wastes in those other days. The man waddled to the swinging gate in the wooden railing and held it open, putting on his customer's smile.

"Come in, Mr. Christian. Come in."

Mont followed him into an office impressive with its roll top desk, its big safe in the corner with the brokerage firm's name in gilt letters across the face. Thomas waved him to a seat and sank heavily into the swivel chair behind the desk.

"What may I do for you, sir?"

Christian said carelessly, "I want you to buy me a hundred and fifty thousand shares of Sandstone at twenty or below."

The broker started. Not that the order was large by Goldfield standards, but after their doubts about Christian, after the news of water in the Emma, it made him wonder.

Certainly Amos Frost was wrong in his guess that the man was a Pinkerton operative. The detective agency went to great lengths to provide cover for their men, but nothing like this.

Automatically he pulled an order pad toward him and made a notation; then he cleared his frog-like throat.

"You have not done business with this office before, have you?"

Christian shook his head.

"Then, if you could give us some credit reference?"

Silently Christian pulled the certificate of his deposit in Nixon's bank from his pocket and laid it on the desk. Thomas picked it up, noting that it was dated as of this day, but making no comment. Instead he said;

"I heard last evening that you have some water on your lease."

Christian nodded, watching the man through half-closed eyes.

"You can't think it too serious, or you wouldn't be buying Sandstone stock?"

"That seems to figure." Christian's tone was noncommittal.

He sat watching the broker fiddle with his pen as the implications ran through his mind, watched the greed that was never far below the surface make the fat throat begin to throb, and could follow the other's thoughts as if they were spoken aloud.

Christian might know something that the rest of the camp did not. Or he might be trying to rig some kind of a stock coup, forcing Sandstone down with the scare of water in the shaft, water that he knew could be managed. Then, when he had bought what he wanted, he might announce an ore discovery. In the way the stock game was played in southern Nevada anything was possible, and things were seldom as they seemed.

Christian held him on the hook for a full minute, then he leaned forward.

"I'm a stranger in Goldfield," he said. "I have no associates. I thought first of going to Nixon and Winfield. In fact that's why I made the deposit at that bank. Then I thought, they're too big for me. They'd eat me alive if they knew what I know."

Thomas smiled hungrily. "They might. It's been done."

Christian nodded. "So I'm going to take a chance with you. I want all the Sandstone stock I can put my hands on. I can't buy all the promotional stock even at the present depressed price. But the water in my shaft will deepen tonight, and tomorrow night and the next, as long as is necessary."

Thomas' reptilian eyes closed, then opened slowly as he got the message. "It only deepens at night?"

"Only at night. If people saw me hauling barrels from the spring in daylight they might ask questions."

A mucous laugh shook Thomas' jowls. "You know, Christian, I thought I'd heard every dodge used to rig the market, but flooding a mine by hand is a new one. There must be something interesting in the bottom of that hole."

"If four or five million is interesting, yes."

Thomas caught his breath. He still did not trust the man across his desk. He trusted no one except Amos Frost, and him only because their interests were identical. But his devious mind could not find a reason why Christian would lie in this manner. But many men, with years of experience underground, had made mistakes about mines, honest mistakes. Finally he said bluntly;

"Why are you telling me this?"

Christian said simply, "Because I need your help. I've already bought fifty thousand shares from Al Pierson, and I have the money to buy another hundred and fifty thousand at twenty, but that's not enough for me. I'm sitting on a fortune and I want to make the most of it."

That Thomas could understand.

"So I'm asking that you buy me what I can pay for, plus a hundred thousand which you will hold for my account. I can pay you for those as soon as I start working the Emma."

Thomas' long, thin lips widened. "You want me to loan you twenty thousand dollars, that's about the size of it."

"That's right. You can hold the stock until I pay for it. But I want it in my name."

"And why should I do this for a total stranger? Frankly, Mr. Christian, you're a man of mystery. No one knows where you came from, or who you really are."

"Does that matter, when there's money to be made?"

"You haven't answered my question. Why do you think I might consider your proposition?"

"Because there's a fortune in it for you. With what I've already told you you can buy Sandstone for yourself. I don't care how much you buy, the more the better, between us we can have control."

"What's to prevent me buying anyway, leaving you out?"

Christian showed him a cold smile. "The minute I think you are not living up to the agreement I am going to ask you to sign, I will pump out the water and tell the world that the vein from the Mohawk runs all the way through Sandstone at a depth of sixty feet. The stock will skyrocket, and your chance to make a killing will vanish."

"Your chance too."

"I already own quite a block of stock, and I control the Emma lease for another five months."

"I wish I could see the bottom of that shaft."

"If you're a good diver you might. But before I dumped the water in last night I took these." Christian drew half a dozen ore samples from his pocket and lined them up on the desk in a neat row.

The man's breath sucked in audibly. His hand, almost webbed, reached forward and picked up one after another of the small pieces, and with a fingernail he traced the line of gold threading through each.

"God almighty. I'd swear this came from the Mohawk. It's better than the Mohawk."

Without answering, Christian reached for a sheet of paper from the stack on the desk and wrote his agreement. Weldon Thomas and Company would buy the required stock, to be held for his account, made over to his name.

"Sign this."

Thomas backed off in his chair. "I'd like to consult with my people . . ."

"Sign it now, if you don't want this find made public."

Thomas signed.

Later, in explaining to Frost and Hickman and Farrel, he sounded awed.

"There's something about this man. You get the feeling that he can force you to do anything he wants merely by his will." He had summoned them to his office to tell the story and exhibit Christian's samples.

Farrel said, "It might be some kind of a con game."

Thomas had little respect for Farrel's thinking, and had often wondered why Frost included the Irishman in their deals. His cheeks puffed out.

"How can we get hurt? We hold the stock as security for the loan. Even if it's all a pipe dream, the eastern leases of Sandstone are paying enough that at twenty cents we can't lose."

Farrel was stubborn. "But why should he hand us . . ."

Amos Frost cut him short. "He's not handing us anything. He's trading his knowledge for stock that he couldn't get otherwise."

"But we couldn't get it all at twenty. As soon as we started buying it would go up."

"Not if we keep harping on the water condition. Weldon says Christian's dumping more in tonight."

Mont Christian was at that moment pouring water down the shaft. They had a bucket line working, from the barrels in the wagon where Matson handed down the full pails to Dick Butler who carried them to Christian, and carried back the empties.

Butler was in his element. The ploy delighted his venal soul, but Lars Matson had been uneasy, had questioned Mont on the ethics of the action. Christian had explained patiently.

"Lars, you and I worked hard to punch that hole down sixty feet, a lot farther than anyone else would have gone. I think we have earned the right to assure ourselves time to buy enough of a voice in the company to make certain our lease will not be cancelled in five months and others reap the rewards of our risk and sweat. When we have what we need, when the mine is opened, then the speculators who only want to profit by our labor, will have their chance."

Now, when they turned the empty wagon again toward the spring, the boy still had a shred of doubt.

"Mr. Christian, how long we going to keep this up?"

Mont's tone was relaxed. "Until we buy all the stock we need or until the shaft is full, whichever happens first."

He slept late that night, had a leisurely breakfast, then returned to the mine, aware that an audience gathered as he passed the other workings. To the end of a dry rope he fastened a head-sized rock and lowered it carefully until it rested on the bottom rubble. Then he lifted it with equal care, stretched the rope on the ground and measured the wet section.

The watchers moved in to examine it. "Still coming in?"

Christian wiped his hands on a linen handkerchief, nodding. "About twice as much as yesterday." He shook his head. "I don't know . . ." He stared at the hole as if he did not know what to do.

Through the next two weeks the Emma mine was the principal joke in Goldfield. The newspaper took to sending a reporter out each morning to report the latest level of the water, suggesting that it might be stocked with fish for Goldfield's dining tables or, if it rose high enough, it might make a swimming hole.

Christian busied himself talking about pumps, but no pump arrived the first week, and when he hauled in the one he then bought from the Mohawk it blew the main cylinder and broke down.

The rumor spread that Christian was trying without success to find a buyer for the lease. The stock fluctuated. Buying strength would appear, gullible eastern money, the town believed, and the price would lift above twenty, but at that price Thomas' agents would lose interest and it would slump again.

No one appeared to want Sandstone. Christian was forced to admire Thomas' procedure, for the broker gradually accumulated the stock without it being discovered. When the price rose above twenty he would dump a block in a wash sale to one or another of his hidden allies.

It took a month before the broker called Christian to the office and spread out the certificates for a hundred and fifty thousand shares. Christian paid for it, complimenting the man, then asked,

"How are you coming with the rest of it?"

"I've got it, in the safe." He rose and brought the sheaf of elaborately designed, richly printed papers, made out in Mont Christian's name.

"I'm having trouble with Al Pierson," he said. "He came to me, wanting to know what we're up to."

"I'll take care of him," said Christian. "How much more time do you want?"

"Give me two more weeks to get ours. It's harder and harder to find. I'm using that list you gave me from the stock book, sending men around the country to buy at private sale from the holders. I'm afraid to use the exchange any longer. It could kick the price too high."

Christian paused in the customers' room on his way out. On the board a block of Sandstone had just changed hands at thirty.

He wondered who was buying at that price. An hour later he had his answer in Al Pierson's office.

The president of Sandstone was unfriendly, even angry, saying in his greeting, "You're sure up to something. Look at this stock book. You cheated me out of my company."

Christian's eyes narrowed. "And you've been buying? Was it you who just paid thirty?"

The man shifted. "I've got as much right as anyone. More. It was my mine in the first place, and you tricked me out of it."

Christian laughed at him. "Al, let's not play the martyr. You bought those claims and issued one million in promotion shares at fifty cents. What happened to that money? You didn't put it into development. You let the leasers do that, and yet there's nothing in the treasury. You put it in your pocket."

The man's mouth worked. "I didn't get it all. The brokers who underwrote the issue got a lot, and there were ten of us in the syndicate. I only got thirty thousand, and I lost that trying to develop some claims up on Snake Mountain. But Sandstone was still my company."

"It still can be," Christian's tone was chill, "If you use your head and keep your mouth shut. You've still got the shares you held out when I bought, plus whatever you've bought recently. What's the total?"

Pierson said reluctantly, "Twenty thousand."

"And in a month that will be worth more than all you sold me. Much more."

The man's face changed dangerously, sharpening with resentment. "So the water is a fake. I knew it. You just wait until I tell the camp." He even rose from his chair as if he would run into the street shouting the news.

"Sit down." Christian said it coldly. "You won't tell anybody anything, for three reasons. Listen to me. The first word you utter will shoot the price sky high and you'll lose any chance of buying more. Second, you are the company president. You like the job, and my combine has enough control to keep you there as long as you behave. Lastly, as president you'd have a hard time convincing people that you weren't in on the secret from the first. Think about it. You won't talk until we're ready." He rose, letting his distaste for the man show, and went out, shutting the door quietly behind him.

CHAPTER
THIRTEEN

Goldfield always loved a laugh, and they never cared whether the joke was on others or themselves. The story of Christian flooding his mine won their hearts to him, eclipsing even the announcement of a new mine that threatened to best the vaunted Mohawk. Throughout the bars and restaurants, the homes and shops Mont Christian was an overnight personality and business leader.

No one censored him for his deception, to Lars Matson's astonishment. The men who followed mining across the West were a special breed, and no one was expected to show his hole card until his chosen time. Even those who had unloaded Sandstone so gladly held a rueful admiration for the man who emerged so spectacularly. Given the same opportunity, they would have done just as he had done.

As soon as Thomas had given him word that he had secured all the stock possible, Christian had repaired the broken pump, sucked the shaft dry and invited the *News* reporters to descend and view the vein. Their story sent the market dizzily up.

Christian put on a hundred miners, drove the cross-cut into the blue rock and within a week was shipping ore. His first mill receipts averaged thirty-nine hundred dollars to the ton. It was a carefully sorted load, and the result ran through the town like a shock. The other leasers on Sandstone ground redoubled their efforts. The hillside came alive. Shafts went down, cross-cuts reached the main vein and production on the whole reef leaped.

The *News* remembered the nickname his first miners had given him, and Lucky Christian became Goldfield's new favorite.

In Amos Frost's household there were mixed reactions. The two children were not surprised: their friend could not be anything except a hero: the grownups were only a little late in discovering it. But they pestered Emma Bondford for an explanation as to why he no longer came to visit them. Emma explained that Mr. Christian was now a very busy man with no time for socializing. She tried to believe this herself, but the last time she had seen him had been the night she had run to him for help and let him see her feeling. Reason told her that he was shying away from any entanglement with her. She fought a constant battle with herself between being powerfully drawn to him and confused over his tactics, which, she admitted, shocked her. María was no help, shaking her head and muttering that Emma had driven off the best man in town instead of making him more welcome.

Amos Frost watched Christian from afar. There was something about the white-haired man that troubled him; yet he could not put his finger on it. He kept away from any personal contact, remaining masked behind

148

Weldon Thomas. More and more, though, he was forced to the conclusion that Mont Christian was a very smart operator and a man willing to make others richer on his own way up. Still hesitating, he grudgingly admitted to himself that he should be making more use of Mr. Christian.

Mont Christian finally forced the issue. He and Thomas' syndicate, if they combined, held enough stock to control Sandstone, yet no mention of such a combination had been made. The Emma was producing the fabulous ore at a steady twenty tons a day. Christian had paid off his loan to Thomas, ordered a steam hoist from San Francisco, replaced the ladders with an elevator, and was pouring money back into development. The shaft was below a hundred feet and he was preparing to drive a second cross-cut into the vein.

He knew that his miners were stealing as they stole from all the leasers, taking much of the hi-grade. He had only to run assays of the vein and compare them with his mill returns to know that, but he did not care. In the cold, bitter logic of his intention, the gold, the money, was merely a tool, a weapon.

But Amos Frost was the spearhead of the group he was after, and Frost continued to elude him. He must, he decided, pull this adversary into the open where he would be as vulnerable as the others when the time came for his final maneuver. For this reason he once more visited the Miners' Bar and presented himself to Sally Ringe.

When Amos Frost arrived routinely, Christian was sitting at the rear table with the woman. The assayer hesitated in the doorway and then came forward slowly. His eyes were on Sally, holding his fury at her for associating with Christian without his permission. On her part, the woman had no chance to explain that she could not have avoided the situation without causing comment at her refusal to accommodate so prominent a guest.

Mont Christian stood up, nodding a greeting. "Don't you think it's time you and I talked together?"

Frost hid his anger instantly, forcing a smile. "Of course. I've been meaning to get around to it, but . . ."

He let the sentence trail off as he turned toward the rear room. Christian went by him and through the door. He was already seated at the poker table there when Frost followed, closed the panel and put his back against it, watching Christian as one poker player watches another. Christian held his eyes until the man came forward and took a chair. They sat thus, looking at each other, until the silence made Frost uneasy.

He shrugged and said with a thin smile, "Drink?"

"Later." Facing the man who had sent him to prison, Christian fought a rising tide of the urge to wrap his hands around the other's throat. He crowded it down, forcing himself to patience. Here was the man he had come to Goldfield to ruin, and had so far made richer. He schooled himself, saying silently, as though he gave himself orders, *Whom the gods would destroy, they first make great.* Then he said aloud, calmly;

150

"Whether or not we like it, we are in Sandstone together. I understand that you hold two hundred thousand shares."

In spite of his control, Frost's head jerked up. He had thought he had hidden his purchases well. He did not know that Al Pierson now cleared every transfer of stock with Christian.

The man from Yuma smiled coldly and pulled a penciled notation from his pocket.

"You," he said, "hold two hundred and sixty-five thousand shares. Weldon Thomas has a hundred and ten and Arnold Hickman fifty-five thousand. A total of four hundred and thirty. Right?"

Frost nodded, wondering what was coming.

"Not control." Christian returned the paper to his pocket.

Frost's lips pulled back in what was intended as a smile. "You don't have control either."

"But I have three hundred thousand shares. I could make a deal with Al Pierson and the rest of the minority holders, which would give me control. But again, you and I together already own more than half the company."

Frost's eyes were cautious. He did not like deals with anyone he did not know thoroughly and could not dominate.

"What's that mean?"

"Why don't we join forces?"

"Just why should we?"

Christian smiled. "Because I have an offer of five million dollars for a majority position in Sandstone."

The words jarred Frost as nothing ever had. "Five million? Who is it?"

"I could refuse to tell you. I could, as I said, deal with the minority group, but that's troublesome, and I have other plans for my time."

He watched Frost's eyes change, grow greedy, and knew that the fish was nosing the bait. But still Frost was not ready to strike.

"Why don't we just sit back and let the mine make us rich?"

Christian said, "Because I'm not that much of a gambler. I've seen mines, promising mines, pinch out. We both know that more money has been poured into the ground than has ever been taken out. I intend to cash in now and move on to something else."

Frost shifted in his seat. "Who are the buyers?"

"An English syndicate. They sent Robert Hodges over here to buy a mine. You know who he is."

Frost said sourly, "One of the top mining engineers in the world, I'd say. I didn't know he was in town." Silently he cursed his spies, who were supposed to keep him informed.

Christian himself had invited Hodges, but he said easily, "He came out to the lease this afternoon and introduced himself. He's been here a week, using another name. He investigated the Mohawk and Red Top, but he says Sandstone is better than either. He knows that if he tries to buy in the open market the stock will go through the ceiling, but if he can get control from us he can hold down dividends, build up the company's reserves and when the leases expire, mine the whole project directly."

Amos Frost was sorely tempted. "You know," he said with a small, deprecating laugh, "I guess I've been wrong about you all along. At first I thought you were a Pinkerton man."

"Sent down here to get you for buying stolen ore."

Frost jumped. "Now, wait . . ."

Christian's smile twisted. "Give me credit for common sense. Everyone in town knows the miners are stealing the leasers blind and selling to the assay offices for a fraction of the ore's worth."

"Yes, but there's never been a suggestion . . ."

Christian made an impatient gesture. "Frost, I don't care who's buying gold. I'm going to buy some myself when I get out of Sandstone."

"You?" Frost could not say why he was so astonished.

"That's right. I'm going to make fifty million dollars before I'm through with Nevada. And the way to make it is not in driving a mine tunnel. The way is by promotion." He paused to let his words sink in, then said quietly, "Ever hear of Snake Mountain?"

It was Frost's turn to be impatient. "A lot of the boys have already been burned over there."

Christian shrugged this off. "I had Dick Butler buy up twenty-seven claims from Al Pierson and his bunch for me."

"Whatever you paid, you got robbed."

"Maybe."

"The only values over there are low grade."

"They were low grade in the Sandstone, to begin with."

Frost snorted. "And you think you'll find another vein like that on Snake Mountain? Things like that only happen once in a lifetime."

Christian's smile was tantalizing. "When I took over the Emma I didn't expect to hit that vein at all. I figured to make my own luck. We went down through sixty feet of county rock without a sign of color."

"You had color at grass roots. You forgetting your bull hide?"

"Am I?"

Frost regarded him with a fixed stare. "Are you telling me you salted that?"

Christian, feeding out just as much of the truth as he needed to make his listener believe, simply looked at the man. Frost frowned.

"Then why did you go on down so far?"

Christian laughed at him. "Use your head. A lot of men have salted mines, but they're always in a hurry, and they only use a few ounces of gold. I brought sixty thousand dollars worth of gold up from Mexico, and I wanted to make a million. I was ready to dig that shaft two hundred feet deep and use all the dust I had salting it. If I could show that I'd taken that much from the lease I'd have sold it for the million, or close to it. People will believe anything after what they've seen in Goldfield."

Frost was nodding rhythmically, reevaluating Christian.

Mont waved a hand expansively. "But I didn't have to go that far with Sandstone, and my appetite's growing. So I'm going to take my profit here and develop Snake Mountain. Listen." He leaned forward, apparently caught up in his project and needing to talk. "I'm going to buy stolen ore, cheap, and run it through my mills. If it takes six months to a year, I'm going to establish a production record that will make them boggle.

"I'll issue fifty million dollars worth of promotion stock, and get a shrewd man like Weldon Thomas to gradually force up the price. I'll pay a dividend, maybe two, maybe a hundred-percent stock dividend. That doesn't cost any money, and all the time I'll be slowly unloading the stock."

Frost wet his lips. His caution was evaporating. He was intrigued. "Isn't there some risk of losing?"

"Where? I make money selling the stock and make commissions on the sales through my broker. I build a separate mill, and issue twice as much stock as it costs. I lay out a townsite. This kind of a mine will attract two or three thousand people. I sell lots to the merchants who want to move in and to the miners. I put in a freight line and a water company, and let the public pay for them. And then, when I've dumped most of my holdings, I'll be gone. And let them look for me."

He stopped the grandiose story. He had sold enough and did not want to oversell. Frost's eyes were glistening at the unfolding possibilities of the swindle. And then, at last, Frost lunged for the hook.

"Christian, I'll tell you what. I'll go along in selling Sandstone to the English crowd if you take me in on this new proposition."

Now Christian apparently backed away. "Why should I? Why do I need you?"

"You need my cooperation to get the English sale, the money for the promotion."

"I can go to Pierson and the minority people instead of you."

Amos Frost felt his chance slipping and resorted to threat. "I could expose you."

Immediately Christian's stony gaze showed him his mistake and hurriedly he turned to selling his worth.

"Christian, I know all the angles to buying the stolen ore you'll need. We can set up a new brokerage house, just you, Thomas and me. And our own bank in the new camp to work through. Let Hickman head that. Farrel can run the water company. You concentrate on the mining end. Let me handle the promotion. I know most of the big men in camp here and they trust me."

"All right," said Mont Christian. "All right." He had trouble keeping a gloating tone out of his voice.

So the Snake Mountain Mining and Development Corporation was born in the unlovely back room of the Miners' Bar. It was a promotion that would shake the mining world, but not even Christian guessed it as he made his way back to his hotel. He looked remote, unsmiling, stern as he moved through the lobby, followed by the whispers that his sudden fame had generated in Goldfield.

CHAPTER
FOURTEEN

The fire of gossip blazed afresh when the English syndicate bought the Sandstone from the new partnership of Amos Frost and Mont Christian. Any new money coming in was good news to the business community, but of even greater interest was the speculation as to what Lucky Christian would turn to next.

Debates raged for a month, and then the announcement burst like a shell. Christian had made a new strike on the flank of Snake Mountain, that isolated, barren slope that had already disappointed so many hopeful prospectors. Lucky Christian he was indeed.

Al Pierson was beside himself. He had sold Sandstone to Christian for pennies, and he had sold his Snake Mountain claims for less. On the morning that the *News* broke the double story he raged into Christian's Goldfield office with blood in his eye.

"Thief," he yelled. "Scoundrel. Cheat . . ."

From the desk where he was composing a list of machinery for the new mine, Dick Butler rose up with a roar, loosening the gun in his belt holster, charging at the invader.

Christian waved him back, winking, saying quietly, "Sit down and stop fuming, Al, you'll blow a blood vessel."

"You're a damn crook." The little man was too wrought up to hear Mont's words. "You sent Butler's bully boys to buy my claims. If I'd guessed you were behind it I'd never have sold."

"Which is why I bought through Dick."

"Bought? Bought? You stole my mines."

Christian laughed at the furious figure. "Al, you had Sandstone and never made a nickel from it except what you stole until I came along. You had Snake Mountain and all you did was lose money there. Now you've made a profit out of Sandstone and you still have an interest in Snake Mountain. Isn't it better to have a small percentage of a producing mine than a hundred percent of nothing?"

Pierson sputtered, but Christian ignored it, his voice friendly. "And there's a place for you in the organization. I'm making you president of the townsite company we've just formed."

Suspicion jolted the anger out of Pierson and his eyes bugged. "Why? Why would you do that now?"

"Because you're the logical man for the job. You know the country up there better than any of us."

Pierson left the office mollified, his enthusiasm beginning to build for his new position, and Butler returned to his chair, shaking his head.

"I just don't get you, Mont. If a man had called me those names I'd have opened him up with a knife. But you give him a title and a salary."

Dick Butler had changed a good deal in the past few months. He had made more money from Sandstone than he had ever expected to have, and with the coming of wealth he had lost most of the bluster that had marked him as a tinhorn. He no longer drank heavily, guarding his secrets. He no longer gambled at the tables, preferring to take an occasional flier in the market, his dress had improved and his voice had lowered. It was as if he were consciously trying to overcome his shortcomings. Without liking him, Christian had found him a useful and able henchman.

"Dick," he said patiently, "a man can make enemies enough without going hunting for them."

He did not add the explanation that he could not afford a man like Pierson running around town calling him a thief. In the swindle he was planning he wanted no breath of suspicion that anything was amiss. Not until he was ready for his grand exposure. For that was his intention. He would build up Snake Mountain out of whole cloth, until Frost's group were inextricably involved, and then reveal the giant deception.

He knew the cost to himself. The identity he had created would be destroyed. He would forfeit everything that had become his. He might even be killed in retaliation by one of Frost's agents. Goldfield would have its joke for fair, but even Goldfield would pull down the principals of a scheme of this magnitude. It was, he felt, a plan worthy of the original Monte Cristo, and now he bent all of the tricks he had learned, all of his energies, toward developing his hoax.

He put Lars Matson in charge of the mining, driving a horizontal haulage tunnel in at the mountain's foot, dropping a shaft to intersect it from the original outcropping found by Pierson's crowd. The ore showed value, but not enough to convince Matson, and he came unhappily to Goldfield to see Christian.

"I'm not a one to suggest that you don't know what you're doing, not after Sandstone, when I thought you were crazy, but . . ."

Christian laughed. "Relax, Lars, and keep digging."

The boy was dogged. "But Mont, the ore we're raising won't average thirty, forty dollars. You can't afford to ship that kind of rock across fifty miles of desert."

"We won't have to. Frost is building a mill, it's already been ordered."

Matson was still not satisfied. For one thing, he did not like Amos Frost. But he was under the spell of Christian's earlier success, so he went back to work.

His doubts were unique in Goldfield. Weldon Thomas had gathered a syndicate of ten leading brokerage houses, and they were industriously selling the fifty million shares of promotion stock. It was issued at forty cents, of which the brokers kept a dime and the rest swelled the company's treasury. Each of the original incorporators had kept a million shares for themselves, and they watched avidly as the issue was oversubscribed and the stock began a gradual rise on the exchange.

Snake Mountain was the talk of Goldfield, but its excitement was as nothing compared to the fever of

160

those who abandoned the parent camp for the new diggings.

The town that Al Pierson laid out along the wide, winding gulch filled and throbbed with life. Along the twisting main thoroughfare, fifty-foot business locations sold at a thousand dollars each. On the side streets, little more than trails climbing the steep mountainside, greasewood-covered cabin sites brought five hundred. An ant hill of activity mushroomed in the middle of nowhere, surrounded by nothing but rock, sand, sparse brush, smothered in dust and heat.

Since the land had cost the Townsite Company nothing beyond the expense of the surveyor and filing the plat at the county seat, that facet of the operation made money from the beginning. With Pierson, Frost, and Christian as officers, it declared a hundred-percent dividend in the second month.

The Water Company, with Hickman as president, Dick Butler as manager, did almost as well. They had built a dam on Squaw Creek below the hot springs and laid pipe thirty miles across the desert and sold all they could to the mine and the thirsty community.

Arnold Hickman brought his bank with him, and around it there sprang up four business blocks of general stores on the ground floor, offices above; a hotel, eight saloons and a red light district. Raw, unpainted wooden buildings and shacks and canvas tents rose in the counterpart of all the mining camps of southern Nevada.

Twenty-five hundred inhabitants appeared to spring from the gritty soil, bragging that there would be five thousand by the end of the year. Unbeautiful as it was, Snake Mountain was born with an immediate pride and a faith in the luck of the man who led it.

Five hundred men were working underground in three shifts. A hundred more raced to raise the mill and mount its centipede of stamps, its engines and gears and belts. A separate crew, long employed by Frost's group for dark missions, dug a storage tunnel into the bank beside the mill. Into this were drawn wagons from Goldfield, loaded with lumber above a false bottom and in the bin below filled with Amos Frost's stolen hi-grade ore. From there the hi-grade was quietly fed into the ore of the new mine. The rich values thus recovered sent prospectors fanning out, clear across the mountain, staking over a thousand claims, whose worthlessness did not in the least dampen the general enthusiasm.

Mont Christian rode the new stage line in from Goldfield and stepped into the dust before the joint bank and express office. His flair for elegant dress alone would have set him apart on this street peopled with begrimed and booted miners, but he needed no such finery to be recognized and hailed by all who passed.

He stood, tall, vital, charged with his strange energy, surveying this product of his mind, the town he had invented, but within him there was no pride in his creation. There was only a checking off of what had been accomplished, a calculating counting of the progress, like the ticking of a time bomb hidden in the mountain.

He waited for Amos Frost to come down from the stage behind him. Frost, who had avoided him for so long, now stayed close to him most of the time. Christian thought wryly that the assayer must fear his new partner would come up with some new money-making scheme in which he would not share unless he was physically present, and he relished the sense of power that he now had over the man. This twisted pleasure he kept to himself, treating his prey with a stern civility that permitted none of them any familiarity. His white head towering over them strengthened the sense of aloofness, and unconsciously they had bowed, accepting his leadership.

When Frost was beside him he nodded at the street. "You see how easy it is to start a boom town."

Frost smiled faintly, all but rubbing his hands together. "And all it's cost us so far is maybe a hundred thousand in Goldfield ore to run through our mill."

"It will cost much more. But we'll have it back when we've sold out. Six months or a year. Have you the patience to wait?"

Frost's eyes wavered, and Christian smiled thinly and twisted the knife with which he now often pricked the man.

"I'll find you something to help you hold on. Take the bags to the hotel while I go see Pierson; then we'll visit the mine."

Frost accepted the lackey's chore without complaint and Christian left him there.

He found Pierson at the townsite office, busy at selling a lot to a saloon man just arrived from Tonopah with a wagon load of whiskey and wanting a main street location on which to pitch his tent. Half the town was still under canvas. The freighters could not bring lumber in fast enough to keep pace.

With the sale completed, the man gone, Pierson cackled happily.

"We're going to have to enlarge the site, business lots are up to fifteen hundred, and one at the corner of Main and Fremont went for two thousand for another hotel. God knows we need that. They're sleeping out in the brush now."

"We also need a post office and a name. I don't want it to be known as The Gulch forever. We'll call it Frost."

Pierson sounded childlessly disappointed. "I was thinking of Pierson. After all, I made the original discovery."

"It will be Frost; he is president of the mine company. And here's something else I want done. Tomorrow a man named Greer will be here with a press and type, to start a paper. Give him a central lot and tell Dick Butler to find enough lumber for a one-room building. I don't care what it costs, but I want the paper publishing by next week."

He left, picked up Frost and climbed the gulch to the mine head. It was dusk when they again came above ground, and Frost was impatient to get down the hill before darkness hid the unfamiliar trail. Christian made an excuse and sent him on ahead, tired of his game of mocking the assayer, wanting to be alone, knowing a restlessness for which he could not account.

164

He sat on a rock and cast over in his mind all that he was doing, why he was doing it. The memory of Lem Travis, who had made it all possible by telling him the secret of the Mexican gold, flicked over him, and Lem's last warning words.

"You'll be sick with vengeance. I'm sorry for you."

He felt no sickness. He felt nothing except the cold fire within him that burned a little brighter as the days marched by, bringing him closer to the culmination of that vengeance.

CHAPTER
FIFTEEN

It was the children who dissipated the mood. As the partners gathered at the gulch, Amos Frost built a rude but adequate house and moved his household to the new camp. In the smaller community young Amos and his sister, roaming loose, soon ran down Christian and dogged his steps. They invaded his office; they heckled him until he took them into the mine; they badgered him until he ran out of excuses and accepted Frost's invitation to dinner.

On the first evening, Emma Bondford's manner was strained, but María joyfully prepared a feast, and Christian more than appreciated the change in fare from the rudimentary restaurants that so far made little attempt to offer more than bare nourishment. As the visits grew more frequent the eastern girl, glad for any company, put out of her mind the strange conflict that she found in the white-haired man. He brought her candy; he was courteous, even friendly. He never referred to the night when she had betrayed her feeling for him. He did not seem to see her as a woman at all, remaining wholly impersonal.

She watched him with Frost and thought she saw a hint that he was toying with the assayer as a cat toys with a mouse. But with the children he was very different. There was obviously a growing affection among the three.

Mont Christian did find a kind of happiness through the next three months, and a relaxation as his plans ran smoothly. As if it were the eye of the storm, a calmness settled in him. Now he had little to do but watch and wait.

The town of Frost continued to boom. Money gravitated to it, money from the Townsite Company, the Water Company, the freight line that brought supplies from Sodaville, the stage line from Goldfield, money that was deposited in Arnold Hickman's bank. Also, they had begun to unload their promotional stock, had collected fifteen million from that, and had spent only about five hundred thousand in development work and salting the mill returns.

To house this horde they had secretly excavated a vault beneath the floor of the bank. Hickman, with a banker's instinct, argued that the golden store should be loaned out at interest, but both Frost and Christian vetoed this, and insisted that the money should be kept in cash, in large bills and dust.

"As little dust as possible," Frost said. "When the time comes to leave we want it in our hands and easy to move. We'll be leaving overnight and we don't want a lot of weight, nor any strings left to track us by."

He had brought Sally Ringe to open a new Miners' Bar, and had laid his plans. They would go to southern France and settle there with the children, use another name, vanish from the wastelands of Nevada.

Christian watched with cold pleasure as the man's impatience grew, and the promise of great wealth swelled his sense of importance. The higher his enemy believed he was, the harder would be the ultimate fall.

He had found, too, that Frost was jealous of the children's fondness for him, as though afraid that he was winning their affection away from their father, and he played on this.

He bought each of them the pony they had been teasing for and the four of them became a familiar sight, riding the mountain through the afternoons, Christian, the Frost youngsters, and their governess. He bought Amos Junior a gun and taught him to hunt through the brush, and he laughed at the boy's pride when he brought home his first quail.

Christian himself had a bag full, but the boy carried his separately, and insisted that María keep track of which was which and serve him that particular bird for supper, and that Mont stay to watch him eat it.

The dinner was good, made easier because Frost was not at home. Christian spent the evening, drawn to watching the play of lamplight on Emma Bondford's hair, and returned to the hotel unconsciously smiling to himself.

He opened the door of his room and stepped in. Then he stopped. Sitting in the chair facing the door a man sat holding a gun on Christian's middle.

It was a man he remembered well, and a shock flashed through Mont Christian.

168

"Hello, Gil Lorran." The voice was as brutal as it had always been. "Remember me? Bob Herbert, from Yuma?"

Of all the guards at the Hell Hole, Herbert was the one most hated. In his middle thirties, not unhandsome, strong and stocky, he had ingratiated himself with the prison officials, and satisfied his sadistic streak by goading, tormenting, mistreating the prisoners until they lashed back; then he would have them beaten.

Christian stood still as the full memory of those years shook through him. In its wake came a terrible frustration. He was so near his goal and here was this apparition raised between him and it. His face filled with a blinding urge to kill.

The guard read it and said hurriedly, "I wouldn't try it. There's a letter in San Francisco, waiting to be opened if I don't keep in contact. It tells them there who you are."

Mont Christian filled his lungs, fighting to control his senses, his impulse. Stalling for time he said;

"How did you find me?"

Herbert's grin spread wide.

"Saw your picture in the San Francisco paper. It said that Lucky Christian" — he stressed the nickname mockingly — "who'd made it big in Sandstone, had an even bigger strike here."

Christian's quick mind caught the meaning. The guard had not come to return him to Yuma. There was still hope. He said levelly;

"How much do you want?"

Herbert nodded, pleased with himself. "You catch on quick, friend. Look at it this way. The prison pays a hundred dollars for the return of an escapee, but that's for river Indians. And there aren't many who get away and find gold mines. I could take you back, but I'd rather have say twenty-five thousand for a starter, and a thousand a week. After that, we'll see. My taste might get more expensive."

Christian's long fingers flexed. They had been curled, aching to close around Herbert's throat. Now relief made him weak and he wanted to laugh aloud. He did not. The solution was simpler than he could have hoped. It would cost money, yes, but money that he expected to lose anyway in the debacle ahead. A small price to pay to insure that his plans were not aborted. But he kept his relief out of his voice.

"All right. In the morning I will get twenty-five thousand from the bank. Then, if you'll leave me your San Francisco address, I'll send you the thousand a week."

Herbert's laugh filled the room. "You'd like that, wouldn't you, if I went away? But I'm not going to. I'm staying right here to watch over my investment. I wouldn't want anything to happen to your health." He paused for emphasis and then added, "Or to mine either. You just remember that letter. If my friend doesn't hear from me for any two-week period, Mr. Gilbert Lorran is going to be discovered living like a king on Snake Mountain, Nevada."

He put his gun away in an elaborate gesture of selfconfidence in his position. "If you don't want to

170

explain having me around you might put me on your payroll. Rich man like you needs a bodyguard, don't he?"

When he had gone Christian lay down on the bed, staring unseeing at the ceiling. It had been a mistake to let his photograph be taken. Frost had insisted that it be used to help the stock promotion, and he had overlooked the danger. He had bought off Herbert, but that was no assurance of security. Someone else might also see it and recognize him, someone less easy to take care of. A chill rage filled him.

Time was running out. If he were to bring down Frost and company from the pinnacle he had been at such pains to build he would have to rush his schedule. Ready or not he must frighten them into seizing the gold from the deep vault and trying to bolt. And he must find a method of sounding the alarm. Ironically, no one would believe him if he tried to tell the town that it was being looted. There had seemed plenty of time for such a device to present itself naturally, but now he felt the pressure of haste to complete his design.

If he had cared for his own safety he could himself have raided the vault and run, but the idea did not cross his mind. He lay there, improvising new plans through most of the night.

In the morning he met Herbert outside the bank, and before they went in told him;

"You're going to have to earn this money. Somebody else may have seen that picture and show up with the same idea you had, or want to take me back. It will be your job to watch and listen and give me warning. Unless you want to lose your meal ticket."

Herbert hitched the gun at his belt and nodded. "That, Mr. Gil Lorran, will be my pleasure."

Christian drew twenty-five thousand from the bank and gave it to the man while Al Pierson looked on. He did not explain. Nor did he explain to Dick Butler when he introduced the prison guard. He said only;

"He will be working with me."

Butler was curious but not disturbed through the first week. Then, as Herbert clung closer to Christian day after day, a jealousy seized him.

Through the months Butler had attached himself to the white-haired man like a stray dog that has found its true master. Christian had made him rich. Obliquely, Christian had changed Dick Butler, cheap saloon bully, insecure two-bit gambler, into a man of substance and confidence. And now this interloper had wedged himself between them. Furthermore, there was a change in Christian himself. He was irritable, more withdrawn than ever. His visits to the Frost house stopped abruptly. He no longer rode the mountain with the kids. Dick Butler set himself to learn the reasons.

His first attempt was less successful for himself than it was for Herbert. He did not question Christian. He invited the newcomer to the Miners' Bar for an afternoon drink and began his probing.

"You an old friend of Mont's?"

Herbert was amused by the question and Butler's obviousness. "I've known him a long while."

"In Mexico with him? You mine with him down there?"

Herbert expanded. "Oh, I was looking out for him long before that. He always needed somebody to take care of him."

While Butler silently agreed that this was what he had been hired to do, Herbert began his own questions.

"I saw him talking to some kids on the street; then a good looking woman came to get them. Did Mont go and marry a widow with a family while I wasn't looking?"

Butler felt a warning bell. So Christian did not confide in this man any more than he did with anyone else. But Herbert could get his answer anywhere along the street, so there was no use in hedging.

"Those are Frost's kids. She takes care of them."

"She's single, huh?" Herbert was genuinely surprised. He had never seen a woman like Emma Bondford, so pretty and a lady to boot. "What's the matter with the men in this camp? I'd think they'd be around her like flies."

That gave Butler a welcome opening, and he took pleasure in saying,

"I guess they're afraid of Christian. Mont could break anybody on Snake Mountain that got in his way."

"Oh? His girl, huh?"

Dick Butler had never comprehended that situation, and had given it little real thought, but he said with certainty,

"That's right."

"Well," said Herbert. "Well, well. Thanks for the drink. I'll be seeing you."

He left the bar, pleased with his discovery. So Gil Lorran had picked up something besides gold since his escape from Yuma, something that looked mighty tasty, and Lorran would not dare protest if he, Bob Herbert, took a share of that too.

He went to his room, dressed more carefully and combed his hair, then he climbed the grade to the Frost house. Emma Bondford believed the message he said he brought from Christian.

"He says he's sorry he's been too busy lately to get up here. He told me to make a call, seeing you're the only lady in town and you must get lonesome."

It was, she thought, one of Christian's kind, impersonal gestures, and these she gathered and hoarded within herself in lieu of what she could not have.

She gave him tea and talked through the afternoon. He came again the next day, and the third day he rented a rig and took her driving. Within that time something happened to Bob Herbert that had never happened before. He fell in love.

He had known many women, but never anyone like this gentle, educated, beautiful creature. And to find that she was lonely was beyond his belief. A dream burst on him. He would marry her and take her out of this country that she obviously was not suited for. With the money he could shake out of Christian he could take her to the dazzling places of the world, give her the luxuries she deserved, live like the mining barons he had read of so long with envy.

All through the drive he watched her hungrily, but he did not propose then. He would do that in the evening, on the porch swing, in proper darkness, when the day alone with him, away from the house and kids had showed her how it could be between them. He talked about the far places that he wanted to see, New York, Paris, London, and saw the starved look in her eyes as she swept them over the empty desert, around the unbroken horizon.

Dick Butler saw the rig go through town on its way out, with the two of them laughing and talking in the shade of the cloth roof. He saw it come back after dark and climb toward Frost's house on the lip of the knoll half way up the hill. Out of his own jealousy of Herbert's closeness with Christian a new suspicion hit him. What was this arrogant stranger doing with Christian's girl? It was one thing for him to be moved aside; Christian himself had a hand in that. It was quite another if the man was trying to make a fool of Mont.

He climbed the hill, circling through the brush around the house and coming quietly down the dark side caught their voices on the porch. He posted himself just behind the corner and peered around, finding them seated in the swing, the light from the living room window falling out across them. He did not hear the full conversation. It had begun before he arrived, but what he heard satisfied him beyond measure.

Bob Herbert, after lifting Emma Bondford to the ground, had reached back, behind the buggy seat, and brought out the box of candy he had stowed there earlier. He stepped up to the porch and waited until she had checked that María had fed the children and put them to bed, until she came through the door again. Then he handed her the box as a surprise.

"Why," she said, "thank you. You're something of a magician. Will you sit down for a moment and taste it before you leave?"

The candy made her think of Christian and wish that it was he who was here, who dropped beside her on the swing, but good manners made her smile and issue the invitation.

Bob Herbert was ready. He leaned forward, looking at her closely.

"You don't get many presents, many nice things here, do you? How long do you mean to bury yourself in this rotten country?"

The question startled her, for she had been asking it of herself more and more often since she had been moved to Snake Mountain. The name itself was offensive. And she had already saved the hundred dollars she had told Christian she needed to leave. She said evasively,

"Why, I don't know. I haven't any place to go."

Herbert felt his pulse pound against his temple. "You can come with me, Emma. I want to marry you. I never asked a woman before. I never saw one I wanted for more than a few hours."

Silent as the sudden moment was, neither of them heard Dick Butler's soft footfall as he reached the corner, and neither noticed the eye that peered around the edge of the house. Emma Bondford was caught in quick panic. But Herbert was bending toward her, forcing an answer. She leaned away, shaking her head, saying the first thing she could think of.

"Oh, I couldn't. I have a job here."

The man laughed, waving the objection away with a hand. "So what? You mean money? I've got plenty, and I can get all the more I want, a hell of a lot more." He caught up the slip and hurried on. "Anyplace you want to go, you just name it. We can live . . ."

"No we can't." She turned her face away, trying to catch her breath. "I'm not in love with you."

"You could be. I can make you. I'll give you anything you want."

As she did not turn back he reached for her shoulder, shaking it harder than he intended, and used the other hand to force her face around, to force his lips against hers.

Instead of responding she pulled further way, and he said in disbelief;

"What the hell's the matter with you?"

"Please. Please." Frantically she used the oldest excuse on which a woman depends. "There is someone else."

In three days he had forgotten whose girl she was supposed to be. Now, instead of releasing her he caught her arms, his fingers biting into her flesh.

"Lorran."

She looked at him blankly, frightened by his voice. The word sounded like an oath.

"What did you say?"

"It's Lorran, is it? You call him Christian." His breath was hard and his voice rose as if its volume would impress her. "You don't even know his name. He's no fit man for you."

She was more and more bewildered, trying to break from the painful grip, gasping.

"I don't know what you're talking about. Let me go."

He was losing her, the one woman he wanted, and in trying to convince her he abandoned all caution and began to babble.

"Mont Christian," he said, "Mont Christian is Gilbert Lorran, a damned killer. He murdered a man down south and was nearly lynched. You can still see the rope burn around his neck. He was sent to Yuma prison for life."

She was shaking her head, the words making no sense to her. "You are crazy. He is here in this camp."

"Sure, because he escaped." The voice was heavier now with building frustration; at himself for giving away his secret, at her for refusing to believe.

Emma Bondford looked at him in horror, a kaleidoscope of swirling horrors.

"It's not true . . . I don't believe it . . . how can you say it?"

His face was almost against hers now, his words a roar in her ears, frantic and careless.

"Because I was a guard at Yuma. I knew him. I was there when he got loose." He ran on, fighting to prove his point. "I recognized his picture in a newspaper and came to make sure. He's paying me a fortune not to expose him. He'll keep paying me all his life. Emma," the voice became a cry, "there'll be all the money we'll ever need to keep us on top of the world."

He threw his arms wide to show her how much they would have. Emma Bondford used her sudden freedom to leap from the swing, to dive past the man and into the house, slamming the door behind her, bolting it closed. Then he was pounding on the door, and she ran into the living room, more frightened than she had ever been.

In the back of her mind she heard the pounding stop, heard heavy footsteps on the porch, and prayed that he was leaving. But the rest of her being was in turmoil. Mont Christian a murderer, a hunted escapee from the dreaded prison. She would not believe it, and yet a small voice told her this would explain the mystery she had always found in him, the total absence of a personal history. And Herbert, what would he do now that he had told her? Would he take Christian back to Yuma? She did not want that. No matter what he had done she did not want that. She wanted him to get away. She must go and warn him as soon as she could safely leave.

The shot echoed in her mind before she realized she had heard it. She had become accustomed to the nightly gunfire from the disorderly saloons down the hill, as she had become accustomed to the many other lurid, raw ways of this wild country. But in the echo she knew that this shot had been much closer than in town.

It was in the very yard. In her distraction she imagined Mont Christian shot and killed by Herbert, lying out there with the guard straddled over him.

She didn't scream, nor even think, but raced through the hall, jerked open the front door and ran across the porch.

There was a man on the ground, and another over him, but as the light poured from the doorway she saw that Bob Herbert was the fallen one. Above him Dick Butler stood, the gun in his hand still smoking.

A new fright caught her. What would Butler, of whom she had been afraid since that day on the Sodaville stage, do now, knowing that she was a witness to this scene? She stood frozen, wondering vaguely why the whole house had not been waked, her mind commanding the children to stay safe in their beds.

Butler looked up to her slowly. She could not believe that he was smiling.

"Got him plumb center," he said with satisfaction.

Emma Bondford fainted.

When she regained consciousness she was lying in the swing with Dick Butler squatted beside her. He was patting her arm, chaffing it, repeating in awkward patience;

"Never mind, never mind, never mind."

Her eyes opened on him, wide, and seeing this he nodded. "He won't bother you again, nor Mont either. You just put it all out of your head."

She lay looking at him and after a moment he got to his feet and turned to the steps. The movement seemed to break her trance and she gave a stifled cry.

180

"Out of my head? I'll never forget a word . . . the shot . . ."

Butler turned back and stood stolid, looking at her with brooding eyes. She was a tenderfoot, for all her months on the desert. She did not comprehend. He said with a gentleness that astonished her,

"What's bothering you, that I dropped him? I got him fair. I gave him his chance, and he drew on me first."

She sat up slowly, reaching out a hand. "But Mont . . . what about Mont? Do you believe . . . ?"

Dick Butler's sigh told of his vast relief. "Oh that. I wouldn't worry about that. You've had a chance to size him up pretty good. I don't know who he killed or why. Whoever it was must have had it coming. Can you figure Christian as a cold-blooded killer, with what you've seen of him?"

"No. No, I can't." There was new hope in her voice.

"Then like I said, just forget it. Just don't mention any of it."

She lifted her shoulders. "Who would I tell? But what if someone heard the shot?"

Butler grinned. "In this town? Who would care? Nobody on Snake Mountain notices a shot after dark. Now you go on to bed and quit worrying."

She obeyed, shakily, despairing that she would ever understand this country, that a man could be shot down at the edge of the town and no one even be curious.

Butler watched her go, priding himself that he had handled the whole situation well. The girl would say nothing. Herbert was dead and his threat to Christian dead with him.

He waited until the door was closed, then got Herbert's rented rig and with some difficulty hoisted the body up and propped it in the seat. He climbed in beside it and turned the horse up across the mountain's face toward one of the early, abandoned, prospect holes. He dumped his cargo unceremoniously into the hole and tossed in rocks from the little dump until it was well covered. With luck it would never be found.

Then he returned the buggy to the barn. The night boy would not know who had rented it. After that he had a single drink in a bar on the way to the hotel, and after midnight knocked on Christian's door.

Christian was not asleep. He let Butler in and listened to the quiet recital. With each revelation he felt himself being stripped naked. His protection was gone now, beyond repair. Oddly it was the girl's knowledge of his record that shook him first.

"She knows the whole thing," Butler said, "but she won't talk."

Christian hardly heard the rambling explanation.

"So you got nothing to worry about," the henchman finished. "You know I ain't going to say anything, and Herbert's safe in that hole on the hillside and in no shape to tell anybody anything."

No, Christian thought, he had nothing at all to worry about. Nothing except time. In two weeks, when Herbert's man in San Francisco received no word from him, the letter would be opened. The manhunt for Gilbert Lorran would begin.

Two weeks he had now to finish with Amos Frost and the other three. Two weeks, before the time bomb now ticking would explode. Was there time for him to bait the final trap and spring it, or was all of the long, elaborate preparation to be destroyed before its end was accomplished?

CHAPTER
SIXTEEN

When Butler had gone Christian sat on alone in the darkness, smiling ruefully at this new irony. Dick Butler had been so smug, so self-pleased at the service he had rendered to his employer. The scamp whom he had first beaten insensible, then threatened, then tempted with the promise of riches into a simulated loyalty, had apparently been bought too well.

Not that Christian believed the killing had been a selfless gesture; alive and free he still meant money to the lieutenant.

Well, brooding on an accident of fate was not profitable. Nor was there profit in waiting any longer to wring the last drop of satisfaction from his vengeance. Any day from now on another who recognized his picture could turn up and destroy the whole design. Mont Christian went to bed and, toward morning, found relief in sleep.

He rose early, and there was no one except the swamper in the Miners' Bar when the Frost associates gathered in the back room in answer to Christian's summons. He had never before called a conference at this hour, and their curiosity was up; yet he was pleased to find that there was no hint of uneasiness among them.

He had this moment of watching them, of knowing what they did not know, of reveling in their arrogant self-assurance. Then he said;

"I got you together to tell you it's time to pull out."

The shock, the protests at giving up their plundering, the outraged questions, fed his pleasure.

"In hell's name, why?" It was Amos Frost. "We've only just got things set up and working smoothly. You said a year . . ."

Christian's lips drew back in a smile that showed his teeth. He must frighten them now, stampede them into running, showing their hands, exposing themselves to the fury of those they had bilked. A posse would find them, catch them with the proof of their guilt upon them, and if he knew the ways of the country as he thought he did he could disappear onto the mountain and from there watch the parading through the streets, the tar and feathering, the eventual hanging of the four. Then finished at last, he could simply fade out of the country.

For the faceless throng who had greedily bought the spurious stock he had no sympathy. By long experience these knew that speculation in mining was at best an uncertain gamble. And for the people who had moved to the town and put their sweat into building it, there would be the recovery of the whole golden horde accumulated in Arnold Hickman's bank. He would take none of it with him. He would take only his horse and blanket and head out like any simple prospector. In none of his planning had he tried to think further than this.

He hid the cold excitement that was rising through him. He looked angry and frustrated and hurried.

"I know I said a year. But we haven't got a year now. Somebody got wise to our operation and we're under the gun."

A long silence held them as the impact of his words jarred them; then James Farrel, with his lack of imagination, swore.

"Somebody here? Let's get rid of him."

Christian did not answer at once, doling out his shocks jealously, then he nodded.

"Hickman, do you remember the morning I paid Bob Herbert twenty-five thousand dollars? That was blackmail money. After that, he wanted a thousand a week to keep quiet."

Farrel let out a gusty breath of relief. "Is that all? I'll have him taken care of in half an hour."

Christian sneered at him. "You're just a little late. He's already dead."

Amos Frost, Arnold Hickman, Weldon Thomas, watched with narrowed eyes, saying nothing, their faster minds running ahead, suspecting Christian's meaning, but Farrel was still obtuse.

"Then what's all the hullabaloo about?"

"I'll spell it for you." Christian's tone had a chill patience. "Herbert was sent here by San Francisco interests who invested heavily in the mountain, to make a private investigation. I don't know how he did it, but

186

he found the hi-grade room. Then he decided to doublecross his people."

"He came to me and told me what he knew and put the bite on me. He also told me that he had written the information in a letter to San Francisco. The letter would be held unopened as long as he reported every two weeks; a nice piece of self protection. But it didn't work. Now, when that letter is read, what do you think will happen to you?"

Farrel's color drained away and he sank onto the corner of the table. Christian watched the perspiration start and glisten on the faces of the others.

Thomas groaned. "Then why the devil did you kill him?"

"I didn't. Dick Butler did, over a personal argument. He wasn't aware of what it meant. In any event, the fat is now in the fire."

Hickman, the banker, said hollowly, "So we have only two weeks . . . and there's a lot of dust we'll have to change into paper . . ."

Thomas, the broker, spoke at the same time. ". . . to call in my brokerage accounts . . ."

But Amos Frost was shaking his head, his eyes on Christian, showing his fright.

"How long has he been here, Mont?"

Mont Christian's smile was thin, cruel. "Three weeks, Amos. And I have no idea when he sent down his report. How much time do you think we have?"

A long sigh came from the group, as if a bellows had caught and squeezed them. Frost gagged, trying to answer.

"Today. Let's clear out today."

Christian's eyes glittered, holding Frost's gaze. "I didn't think you'd panic, Amos. Where's that cool head of yours? We can't get ready today. Or are you going to cut and run and leave all that money behind?"

For a long moment no one spoke. With a single accord they now turned to Christian to lead them out of this danger, to keep their stolen fortunes intact.

He was silent, enjoying watching them squirm, until Farrel blurted belligerently,

"You got us into this, Christian, now get us out."

Christian still took time, looking for a long while at each of them as if for assurance that they wanted his advice, and finally he lifted his shoulders and dropped them.

"I think we'd better shoot for tomorrow night. Amos, tell your family you're taking them for a vacation to San Francisco. Tell them to pack light and get them out of here this afternoon, have them wait for you in Sodaville."

"Farrel, pick five drivers, have them ready with their hi-grade wagons. Hickman, tonight you divide the currency and dust in the vault five ways and get it packed to move."

"Today we'll announce that we're shutting down the mill for a few days to install more stamps, and shipping ore to Sodaville until we open again."

"Tomorrow night we'll pull the wagons in behind the bank, load from the vault into the false bottoms, then go on up to the mine and fill the beds with ore, one wagon for each of us. We'll go to Sodaville, dump the ore at a mill there, then drive on to the railroad, put the money aboard the train and be long gone. Arnold, be sure you make those packages look like regular baggage."

"Once we're in San Francisco we can split up, get a steamer out of the country or go wherever we want, but I suggest that it be a long way from here."

He watched the fear leave them as each began to lay his plans, as their sense of safety began to reassert itself, and was satisfied. He wanted them frightened enough to run, but not to bolt, and not to suspect the trap.

Mont Christian followed them out of the Miners' Bar, leaving only Amos Frost to alert Sally Ringe to prepare for the sudden departure. His lips thinned down with a fresh anger at Frost, knowing that the assayer intended sending the saloon woman out with his children, that he expected Emma Bondford to submit docilely and accept Sally Ringe as her mistress, expected his son and daughter to accept her as their foster mother.

It would never come to this, of course. They would wait in Sodaville until the news came of the debacle on Snake Mountain. Then Emma and Amos junior and Peggy would be free of the evil influence that now dominated them.

He stopped suddenly on the sidewalk and stood staring up the street. A new coldness went through him like a wind. He did not hear the greetings of the crowd that jostled around him. He was more alone than he had ever been, seeing sharply that in his single-purposed stalking of his enemies he had forgotten something of importance. The children, Emma, were innocent of any quarrel with him. Yet by tomorrow night the three would be abandoned, stranded in Sodaville, Nevada, with neither friends nor money.

He cursed himself. There had been plenty of time, through the long-played game, that he could have set up a trust for them in San Francisco. He had not done so. Money had meant nothing to him beyond a weapon for his use. He had had it in abundance. He had used it extravagantly. In wry chagrin he knew that he had overlooked its necessity to normal living.

Now there was no time to set up such a trust. His time was run out. But perhaps not quite. In more haste than he had known for many months he turned toward Arnold Hickman's bank and caught the man as he was going through the door.

"Arnold," he said, "I want ten thousand in currency out of my cut, now."

The banker swung around, first in surprise, then suspicion pinched his face. "That's a lot of money, Christian, what's it for, more blackmail?"

In his hurry Christian felt off balance. Beneath his breath he swore again, knowing that he had fumbled, that he must convince the banker that all was well. He forced a smile.

"Nothing like that this time. It's a small present to leave for a friend who won't be going with us."

He held his breath while Hickman thought this over, until the man's mouth turned down in tight scorn.

190

"Butler?" Hickman guessed. "I'd say you'd paid him enough. I didn't know you had a sentimental bone in you."

Christian smiled in quick relief. "Part of my vanity, Arnold. I like to pay a little more than just my debts."

He waited for the man to count out the bills, to mutter that it was spendthrift foolishness. He took time to caution that the gesture was not to be mentioned to anyone, then headed for his room at the hotel.

He wrote a short note, making no explanation, only directing that Emma Bondford should use the funds to keep herself and Amos Frost's children. Then he wrapped the whole in a bundle and made his last call on the house on the hillside.

The youngsters thought the bundle was a present for them and tried to wrestle it from him, and he wished that he had indeed brought them a gift, wondering at the twinge of regret that he would not see them again. But he put this aside. He had other work to do that afternoon and the hours were beginning to crowd down on him.

"Amos tells me he's going to take you on a vacation," he told the girl. "Take this with you, but don't open it until you're in San Francisco."

She looked at him anxiously, put out her hand as if to break the long silence between them, to talk of Herbert's accusation, but he gave her no chance. He nodded at María, in a flurry of packing, rumpled the children's heads and laughed.

"I see he's already told you. Have a good trip."

He turned away and heard the girl's voice behind him, sagging and resigned.

"He just left. He hasn't been gone fifteen minutes . . . thank you for the package . . ."

He waved a hand without looking back, taking the road up the hill, already thinking of the steps he must take now.

When there had been time, he had intended to use Lars Matson to trigger the discovery of the swindle. Matson was a good miner and already mystified that the ore he took from the mine produced such values. Christian had watched him closely, in no hurry for the day when the boy would begin to suspect, would on his own send samples of the rock to Goldfield for an independent assay and discover its barrenness.

Lars would then come to him for an explanation, he knew. That he had not done so thus far was because of the spell of the surprise luck in Sandstone, his almost superstitious belief in Mont Christian who made riches so magically.

But Lars Matson was deeply honest. It had cost him a bout with his conscience to take part in the flooding of the Emma mine after the valid discovery. Christian had argued him into accepting a rationale for that, but he knew that Lars could not remain quiet when he learned the secret of Snake Mountain.

The fuse had been long. Lars would be slow to arrive at the point of doubting his hero, slower to take the physical step of seeking proof. Now the fuse was too long; Christian could wait no longer. He must force the discovery.

He climbed to the mill, walked through it casually and turned the corner, following the corridor where hand tools were kept, to the locked door at its dark end. He took a miner's lamp from the shelf, lighted it, found the key deep in his pocket and opened the lock. Inside were the bins holding the latest shipment of the rich Goldfield hi-grade. He chose a double handful of the finest samples and carried them out, locking the door behind him.

Later, he found Dick Butler in town and sent him to locate Lars Matson.

"We'll have dinner together," he said. "I've got something to tell you."

The restaurant was far from as sumptious as the Palm Grill, and the bar whiskey was raw, but Christian, with an air of celebration, ordered a bottle brought to the table. Butler, with his new care, drank sparingly and Matson habitually took a single glass. Mont Christian, though, seemed uncommonly thirsty.

As they ate he grew gayer than they had ever seen him, winking mysteriously, apparently savoring whatever news he had for them, and only over coffee did he lean forward and lower his voice.

"Tomorrow," he said, "I want both of you to go to Goldfield and sell out your Snake Mountain stock."

Butler's eyes rounded. "Sell out? Now? What for?"

Again Christian winked. "This is just between us, but we, the officers, have a deal on the fire to sell out the whole works. We're going down to San Francisco tomorrow night . . . with the shipment to Sodaville . . . to talk to a syndicate that wants to buy. If we sell, the stock will drop until people see what the new owners will do, and I want you two out while the price is up."

Matson watched him quietly, but Butler swelled indignantly.

"What do you want to sell out now for? There's more money coming out of this mountain than any of us ever saw. It's too good a thing to let go of."

Christian wavered slightly in his chair and grinned, a somewhat foolish grin.

"Time to get out is when a thing is good. Never can tell when a vein will fault, or pinch out and leave you holding an empty sack."

He spilled some coins on the table clumsily and made an effort to stand up, but abruptly dropped back, shaking his head. Both of them stared at him. They had never before seen this man drunk, but plainly he was unable to handle himself now.

"Lars," Christian reached heavily for Matson's arm. "Lars, gimme a hand. Help me get up to bed. Must be the excitement . . ."

Butler rose to assist from the other side, but Christian waved him off, his voice slurring.

"Let's not make a parade of it. I don't need an army."

Butler did not like the rebuff, but he stood as ordered and watched Lars Matson steer Christian on a laborious course to the street and turn him toward the hotel.

Matson, confused but sympathetic, led the man he idolized as he would lead a child, helping him climb the hotel stairs and find the proper door. Here Christian leaned against the wall, fumbling through his pockets, muttering half aloud;

"Key . . . the key . . ."

He found the key to the hi-grade room, tried it in the lock and weaved back in disgust.

"Wrong key. Here." He thrust it into Matson's hand, dredged up the hotel key and passed it over too. "You open the door, Lars. I've got to lie down . . ."

Lars Matson fumbled in his hurry, then shoved the panel inward and put his arm around Christian, supporting him into the room and to the bed. Christian leaned perilously close to losing his balance, made a swipe with one hand for the pillow and swept it away, with the other hand reaching to yank down the covers. Then he sank on the side of the bed and dropped his head into his hands, anchoring his elbows on his knees.

He sat there, breathing heavily, a man fighting for control, and did not look up to see Matson's eyes as they widened on the cluster of ore samples nested beneath where the pillow had been. The tell-tale, blue ore, unmistakably from the Mohawk.

It made no sense to Matson, the handful of rocks being hidden there, but he was too concerned with Christian's condition to wonder long. He looked from them to the bowed white head, put his hand on Christian's shoulder and tried gently to ease him back onto the bed.

Christian resisted, grunted, flung the hand away, and then in a quick movement swung around and scooped the bits of ore beneath the cover.

"Lemme be. Go on. Get out of here."

Matson backed away, more curious than worried. "Mont, what's the idea?" Then to prevent the drunken man's taking offense, he tried to be funny. "What are you trying to do, hatch those samples?"

Christian looked up, the foolish grin again spreading his lips, and giggled. "That's right, hatch em. Hatch the old Mohawk right here on Snake Mountain. That's good, Lars. Here," his voice brightened and his hand scrabbled beneath the blanket, bringing out the rocks, tossing them one at a time toward the boy.

"You want em? Take em. Maybe you can hatch em as good as we did. We got a bank full, real full." He appeared to think for a moment, then nodded at Matson's hand. "That key, important key. Key to hatchery. Won't need it after tomorrow night. You keep it. You been a good boy, Lars, a good boy. So long . . ."

He closed his eyes and leaned slowly back until he lay uncomfortably curled on the bed. His muscles went slack, and in another moment Mont Christian began to snore.

He waited until he heard the door open and close, waited still awhile to be certain that the boy was gone, then Christian rolled, opened his eyes and looked around the room. Once more he had set in motion the cogwheels of events, moving them in the direction he had chosen. Inexorably now his vengeance would walk down upon his four targets.

He counted off time enough for the boy to get a good head start, then he rose, remarkably sober, and went down to the street. He turned uphill, and as he passed the last straggling house saw the shadow of a body moving in the darkness ahead of him.

He kept the distance between them, and stopped when the figure stopped, as Matson hesitated between the road to the mine and that of the mill. But Matson knew the mine inside out, its shafts and tunnels and vents. There was nothing there that a key might unlock. Yet he took that way.

Christian followed, puzzled now, until at the entrance a miner's lamp flared, and he knew that Lars had needed light. He faded into the bushes as the light came toward him and passed, and turned into the other road.

Following the afternoon's announcement, the mill had been shut down. There was no light there, nobody in the cavernous shed. Christian halted outside, watching as the small glimmer told him that Matson was moving slowly down the aisles, thinking, figuring where a hidden storage place might be. Then the light disappeared in the area of the corridor.

For a long while there was neither sound nor movement, only the lurking massiveness of the silent stamps. Then the little light glowed again, came forward very slowly and Lars Matson, holding the miner's cap with its lamp in his hand, stepped through the entryway. Christian, waiting behind a boulder, had a brief look at the young face, contorted, fighting tears, and knew that he had destroyed this boy's faith.

Again his singleness of purpose had led him to hurt an innocent person. It was a by-product that he resented, regretted, but this would be the last time.

Lars would go with his news to someone, probably Al Pierson, who had been elected mayor of the town. They would gather a posse and at midnight tomorrow close in on Amos Frost's venal clique as they transferred the great fortune from Hickman's bank vault to the secret bins below the wagons' floors. Soon, then, it would all be over. Never again would any of the four be able to condemn a man to the slow death of Yuma Prison.

CHAPTER
SEVENTEEN

Mont Christian returned to the town, seeing the main street that pitched below him nearly deserted at this hour, its path picked out of the gloom by the lighted windows of the saloons and gambling halls.

He passed the dark hulk of Amos Frost's house, the straggling cabins of the head of the street, and reached the livery stable, a block from his hotel. Here a paw of the mountain stretched down, creating a twist in the gulch, and the hostler had used the terrain to his advantage, cutting back into the bank so that he needed to build only two sides for his corral.

Christian ordered the night boy to bring up his horse, saddled it himself, and then watchfully rode on down the street. There was a bare chance that Lars Matson had already alerted someone, although he did not really expect it. He had been at pains to establish the time and place of the decampment in the boy's mind, and the suspicion of what was planned.

No one stopped him, and he turned the horse into the narrow alley beside the hotel, leaving it in the small rear yard that, like the corral, had been gouged out of the mountain.

He used the rear outside stairs to the upper hall and found his room, packed a slender saddle roll and was gone within half an hour.

He saw no one, crossing the main street and turning into the darkness of the back ways. Then he was on the mountain, threading upward toward an outcropping of boulders that overlooked the winding street and the alley that ran behind Arnold Hickman's bank.

There he would wait, well hidden, where he could watch the next night's conclusion of his machinations.

He curled in his blanket and spent his first night on the ground since he had left Mexico. In the morning he built a smokeless fire and made coffee. He wanted nothing to eat. His stomach muscles were tightening, squeezing out hunger.

Through the day he sat all but motionless, watching the movement in the town, judging it for sign of unusual activity. Miners appeared from their shacks, making their way up to report on schedule at the shaft house. A skeleton crew of cleanup men turned toward the silent mill. At the Miners' Bar the swamper came through the door to empty his pails into the gutter, paused in the early sunshine to scratch his ribs, and went back inside.

At nine o'clock Al Pierson strode importantly from his house and opened his office, and almost on his heels Lars Matson, his yellow hair rumpled and bright in the early light, turned in at that door.

Christian smiled.

Ten minutes later the two came onto the street together and walked hurriedly to the hotel where

Christian had lately lived, and after another short wait they appeared again. They turned toward the livery, and after that separated, going in opposite directions, but neither venturing toward the bank, Thomas' brokerage house nor any of Amos Frost's haunts.

Throughout the day Lars Matson stopped one and another man, who then went directly to Pierson's office. Christian counted a dozen and was satisfied. At midnight, when the wagons were drawn up behind the bank there would be, besides the partners, the five drivers, hardcases all who had long ago been bullied or blackmailed or paid to do the group's bidding. If they chose to fight to protect their masters, the twelve possemen should be sufficient to handle them. But more likely, in such a situation, they would be offered amnesty to leave or simply fade away on their own. They were not important even though they might be surprised as they carried the cases of money from the building.

At ten o'clock Arnold Hickman brazenly opened his bank and Thomas his brokerage. The hours slipped by in a business-as-usual air.

The mine shifts changed. The street filled with men on their daily errands. Dick Butler sought Christian in the hotel and came out to look uncertainly up and down the block, then went to open Christian's office and wait there for Mont's accustomed arrival.

Christian fed his horse, stretched his legs with a short walk through the brush, and returned to his vigil.

Evening crept in, the long shadows gathering first on the floor of the desert as the sun dropped behind the ragged western peaks, turning their slopes blue and sliding up the eastern face to swallow the town of Frost. Christian could see little against the blazing glare until the fireball sun was gone, then his eyes adjusted to the short desert twilight, and he could follow movements again.

Lights winked on. The restaurants and saloons filled. Men became dark shapes that vanished in the spaces between the glowing windows. The mine shifts changed again, and the town filled up. It seemed to Christian that fewer men than usual left the gathering places to seek their cabins, but he thought little of it until the moon, rising behind his back cast the street in a pallor that again illuminated the whole area.

It was, he judged, close to midnight. Hardly surprised, he saw Sally Ringe's buggy at the rail before the Miners' Bar, and in the alley behind the bank the shadowy forms of the five wagons climbed, turned around, and stopped in a train. He could make out a dim flickering of dark shapes moving from the building to the wagons and knew that the horde was being loaded.

A surge of panic touched him that he had misread the signs of the day. What if Lars Matson had struggled with his conscience and decided that his debt to Mont Christian was greater than his duty to his fellows? What would he do if Frost led his entourage down the hill toward the Sodaville road without being discovered? Would he even be believed if he rode into town and tried to sound the alarm?

He fought to quiet his nerves, now drawn taut, telling himself to wait. Then he was both relieved and freshly worried to see a slow but general exodus from all the lighted doorways and a gathering of a crowd in the dust of the road.

There was no sound. There was a milling of shapes and then the body of figures divided, one part moving down toward where all of the streets ran into the single trail that led out of the gulch, the other flowing upward toward the bottleneck at the head of town.

So it was not to be a posse, but a general rising. He did not like this. A posse could act in an orderly fashion, accomplish its work and disband. But a crowd such as was growing down there could become a danger. Coming from the saloons, many of these men would be drunk, and it took only a little to ignite a mob. If that happened, if violence broke out and spread there would be people hurt. A mob knew no reason, and its targets could change like mercury. He had never imagined nor intended a reaction of this size. But it was there. And as the crowd shape ebbed toward the streets that flanked the bank, he heard the noise begin, the growl like a distant surf that rose on the night air.

Then suddenly he was on his feet, he was yelling, waving his hands. On the white ribbon of road below him the shadowy shape of Amos Frost's carriage disengaged itself from the bulk gloom of the house and turned downhill. On the seats he could make out two larger figures, two smaller, and knew instantly that Frost, for some reason of his own, had not sent his family out as he had been told to do. Now they were driving down into the fury that they could not see from behind the mountain's nose, unable to hear his shouts of warning.

Christian did not take time to saddle his horse. He caught up the bridle, flung himself on the animal's bare back and struck his spurs into its flanks, careless as it lunged forward through the shadowed brush that at any step it might drop a hoof into a gopher hole and break both their necks.

He took the shortest way toward the road and turned into that, bent low over the racing animal's neck. But he was too far away to reach the carriage before it turned the corner and came against the group of men climbing to cut off retreat in this direction. He heard the growing rumble of angry voices and slowed his headlong pace, not wanting to burst upon them without knowing what was happening.

But even drunk, these miners had no quarrel with women and children. As Christian turned the curve around the knoll, they were parting, giving the carriage passage, otherwise ignoring it, continuing uphill, cutting him off from it. He would be recognized and pulled down if he tried to ride on.

He sat, frantically trying to find a way of reaching the carriage, and then a new noise reached him. There was a volley of gunfire from behind the bank. Grimly he watched the carriage move on without pause. Gunfire was too common here to be noticed.

But as if in answer to his need the crowd coming toward him turned, hesitated, and then flowed back, taking to the side streets, running toward the sound of shots.

Christian waited no longer. He raced after the carriage, toward the jaws of the trap that he himself had set. Ahead of him the other segment of the mob had also turned, was sweeping back and spreading to join the fight as its volume swelled.

There was no way now to get the carriage free of town. The best he could think of was to overhaul it and find some shelter for its passengers. He caught it close to the hotel, caught the team's reins and yanked them to a stop. The urgency in his voice cut short Emma Bondford's surprised protest.

"Don't argue," he shouted. "Get down, get down all of you. Get in the hotel. Run."

As he gave the order he flung himself to the ground, reaching up his arms. "Give me the youngsters. Hurry." And as first the girl and then the boy were handed out to him he set them on their feet, swatted them and again shouted, "Run."

María scrambled with a heavy grace from the rear seat and ran after the children and then Emma Bondford, not knowing why she obeyed so hastily without reason, accepted Christian's hand and raced at his side up the step and through the door.

Christian stopped only to slam the door, to glimpse the horses, spooked by a new fusillade and a roar of shouts, rear and bolt, dragging the carriage on a jolting, dizzy dash down the street. Then he was herding the group through the empty lobby, detouring to blow out the lamp on the high desk, calling through the instant darkness;

"Through the kitchen. Into the pantry, the storeroom."

With long strides he led them through the dining room, dodging furniture by light of the moon as it filtered through the front window, into the dim kitchen and across it to the door of the storeroom. It was the safest place he could think of. Dug into the bank for coolness, all except its one wall were of earth, for a thick dyke had been left between the room and the little yard. He found a match in his pocket and lighted the candle beside the door.

In its glow he looked at the round, frightened eyes of the boy and girl, at Emma Bondford's breathless bewilderment, at María's surprising lack of concern. The Mexican woman was already rearranging the sacked potatoes, making places to sit down, seeming to expect a long wait here. Before the eastern girl could find her voice, he said;

"I'm sorry this happened. But there's going to be trouble outside, a lot of trouble. Don't any of you leave this place."

He was gone then, threading his way quickly to the front window and peering out. In the little time it had taken him to get his charges indoors the street had emptied as men ran to the rear of the bank. Now it was filling again, below and above. The crowd was moving back cautiously, closing off the road at both ends of the block. He guessed that after the skirmish behind the bank Frost's men had barricaded themselves in the building, that the mob was now moving to surround it, to drive them out and into its hands by either the rear or front doors.

Almost at once the front door opened and in a concerted rush the partners came out, bent low, running directly toward the hotel. Immediately behind them came the drivers, pausing to snap shots both ways along the street. Firing from the mob answered them, yells and shouts. One running figure threw its hands in the air and pitched forward. Another crumpled and rolled. The mob surged forward. The hotel door crashed open and a tangle of bodies tumbled through.

In the darkness Christian could not tell who was inside. He did not care. His thoughts were only of the huddled children, the women in the storeroom, the likelihood that this building would be rushed. He turned again to the window.

The crowd outside had moved up, moved into a half circle across from the hotel. Torches were being lighted now, spreading their red glow over the heads, lighting the faces. Christian recognized half a hundred whom he knew, good men, solid miners, merchants, businessmen who had believed in him and established themselves in this town, men who had gone out of their way to smile and speak to him.

Now, theirs were the faces of anger, of hatred, the face of vengeance, all destructive. And in them he saw his own face at last. He saw the beast he had unleashed. He heard Lem Travis' dying voice repeating, vengeance destroys the avenger first.

For all of these years Gilbert Lorran had lived with a dream of death. The dream included himself, for he had envisioned no future, nothing beyond this night. Now the night had betrayed him.

The shell that he had cast around himself broke. Horror at what he had done, like bile, swept its bitterness through him. Emotions that he had believed dead shook him dizzily. The children in the storeroom, what they had come to mean to him, the blonde woman there, whom he had put into this danger, the powerful need of her, all that he had shut away from him rushed over him now.

He would give his life, life that had sudden meaning, to undo the monstrous months. But that could not be done.

In the room around him there was stumbling confusion, curses from those who had made their way inside. These had been his enemies. Now, to protect the lives in the storeroom he must try to protect these men. He shouted orders to cover the windows and was strangely relieved to hear Frost answer, to know that at least the children's father lived, that they need not yet face the trauma of his death.

"Amos," he said, "your family is in the storeroom back of the kitchen. They're all . . ."

He was cut off as shots crashed one window, spilling the glass into the room. He swung, pulling his gun, but did not fire. From somewhere outside Al Pierson's voice came to him.

"Christian, if you're in there, take a look. We've got enough men to handle you all. You, Frost, Thomas, Hickman, come out and we'll let the others go."

"I'll come alone." He called it through the shattered window. "Be satisfied with that. You don't want a massacre."

The offer was drowned in a roar of voices, and one raucus laugh rose from deep in the crowd.

"We want the lot of you, clean out the rats. I'll count to ten, then . . ."

The count began. Then suddenly a man jumped from the wing of the mob and ran toward the door. Christian almost shot him, then saw in the dancing torchlight that it was Dick Butler and shouted;

"Get back . . ."

But Butler plunged through the doorway and crouched at Christian's side, panting. "Hell with it. We can hold those drunks off all night."

His gun exploded and a figure in the mob jerked and fell. Frost's crowd picked up the fight, and the thing that Christian was trying to prevent erupted. A battle was joined, involving the whole street.

The mob split, retreated, hunting for shelter between the facing buildings. Half a dozen men were left lying unmoving in the dust. Behind him Christian heard the cry and the falling of one of that force.

There was a temporary lull during the regrouping outside, and in the lull a new crash of glass signaled that something had been hurled through an upper window.

A moment later Christian was knocked from his feet by the force of a blast as the dynamite bomb exploded upstairs.

He heard panic in the shouts around him as he found his feet, heard Dick Butler's defiant shout and well-placed shots that drove back a scattered rush. Through the window he saw a red glow spread across the leaping figures, heard the shout of fire, and knew that the bomb had set the upper story of the wooden building blazing.

CHAPTER
EIGHTEEN

The fire gave a moment's respite to the group trapped in the hotel as the rush that had started faltered and turned back to the safety of the alleys. Now the street was deserted except for the dancing red anger that reflected from the opposite windows. Crimson streaks raced like an aurora borealis across the walls, seeming to bring the buildings into leaping life.

Christian spun around, using the baleful light to make a fast survey about him. Frost and Thomas crouched behind the desk, staring toward the crackling sounds above them. Arnold Hickman sprawled on his back, something in his posture telling that he was dead. Farrel nursed a broken arm, past fighting, and the two teamsters who had made the rush inside were now crawling for the door, jerkily waving white handkerchiefs before them. Only Dick Butler still held his ground, crouched beside the window, methodically reloading his smoking guns, and to him Christian called.

"Frost's children and two women are in the storeroom. They'll roast if I don't get them out before this place collapses. Can you hold this door for five minutes?"

Butler grinned up at him. Christian had never seen the man more confident.

"I'll hold her until she burns around me."

There was not time to express his rush of gratitude nor the pain of the irony that it was this man for whom he had had so little respect who was in these final moments the only one on whom he could depend. Christian was already moving away, calling over his shoulder,

"I'll be back as soon as I get them clear."

"Don't bother."

The voice caught him as he reached the dining room, its tone telling that Butler did not expect him back, that he had already accepted the end. Christian shook the surge of self-accusation from his head and ran on.

At the kitchen door Amos Frost caught him, his tone tight with fear.

"I heard . . . the kids."

All across the room the footsteps, the babbling, dogged him. "We got to get them out . . . it'll be an oven in there . . ."

Then Christian was at the storeroom door, jerking it open, almost running down Emma Bondford. She stood just inside, her arms around the shoulders of the children who clung tightly to her, her face bloodless. He caught her arm, pulling the three of them into the kitchen, shoving them toward the rear door. As they stumbled toward it María rose calmly from her seat and followed, as though she were long hardened to flying bullets and leaping flames. And still Frost gibbered.

212

"It's over our heads . . . the fire . . . the ceiling will come down any minute."

Christian turned, caught the assayer's shoulder and pushed him through the door into the little rear yard. It was less than twenty feet square and already the heat there was choking as flames licked out along the rear eaves. The banks cut out of the mountain paw were too steep to climb, and the alley was impossible. But on the right the brushed surface was only ten feet high and at the top a large rock hung, imbedded in the rim. Christian prayed that it was solid.

There was no ladder, and he spun back into the kitchen, running for a small table beside the big range. He caught it up, twisted it sideways through the door and ran to set it against the bank, yelling at Frost.

"Get up. Get up."

Frost appeared not to understand, and Christian grabbed his arm, hurled him toward the table, climbed to its top and hauled Frost after him. Under their combined weight the table lurched and Christian prayed again. He put his back against the bank, steadying the legs somewhat, and made a saddle of his clasped fingers.

"Come on. Up. Move."

Frost got the idea then. He put one boot into Christian's hands and Mont swung him up, pushing on the stiffened legs until Frost's clawing fingers closed over the edge of the rock. Then pulling himself, boosted by Christian's extended arms, he got a knee over the rock and rolled onto the ground behind it.

Christian spared a glance toward the burning building where the flames now leaped above the curling roof. His face felt the blast of heat, but at least the smoke and fire screened them from the watching eyes across the street.

Wordlessly he reached down, pointing at the little girl whose head was buried in Emma Bondford's skirt, and instantly the eastern girl scooped up the child and lifted her. Christian pulled her to him for a moment, reassuringly, saying;

"Stand on my shoulders, honey, and reach high. Your daddy will pull you on up."

Whimpering, the child climbed. Christian caught the small ankles and hoisted her until he felt Frost take her weight, then he reached for the boy. Amos junior came up to the table, his eyes filled with terror but also with absolute faith in his white-haired friend. He even grinned as he was half thrown upward.

Then María shoved Emma Bondford forward. Christian caught her hand, swung her to the table, gripped her below her knees and raised her into Frost's grasp, got his palms beneath her feet and pushed her upward.

María was a greater problem, her weight making the table wobble and twist, yet it held as Christian bent, as she scrambled up his back, her moccasined feet found his shoulders and she clawed like a climbing cat, helping him to stand upright. She stepped up to his head, then Frost had her hands and she dug her toes into the bank, walking up until she was rolled to safety.

That effort cost Christian most of his strength and he stood panting, looking up the bank. Three feet separated his stretch from Frost's downreaching hands, and he knew that he could not make the climb without help. Now the heat beat at him with scorching intensity and Frost yelled down with hopeless urgency.

Mont Christian shook his head. "Go on. I can't make it. Go on. Clear out."

Emma Bondford swung her arm, pointing, speaking for the first time. "In the storeroom. There's a rope."

Christian looked that way. There was blackness behind the kitchen door, smoke roiling from it, but there was no flame yet. He leaped from the table and made the dash. He found the rope and started back, and then remembered Dick Butler and turned. But the way was closed, the dining room a coiling mass of licking fire, there was no chance.

Again he swung toward the only exit left, and as he jumped, a section of the kitchen ceiling fell, showering live embers across the room. He leaped through it, feeling the searing through his boot soles. Then he was in the yard, shucking out of his coat as it smoldered, throwing an end of the rope toward Frost.

"Cinch it around the rock."

He tied the other end around himself, no longer trusting the strength of his fingers, then, leaning back against the rope on which Frost pulled, he slowly walked up the cutbank, rocked over on his knees and hands at the top, and needed to rest there for long moments, taking stock.

María had shepherded the children up the steep mountain face, out of range of the spreading heat. Frost, now that Christian was safe, scrambled after them, but Emma Bondford waited, her face crimson under the fire's blast, until Christian made the effort to rise. Then she caught him beneath his armpit and tugged until he gained his feet.

Only then, as they climbed, grabbing at brush to help their ascent, did she ask a question.

"Mont, what's happening? What is it all about?"

He looked at her, the agony of his recent revelation distorting his face, haunting his eyes.

"It's my fault. I did it. I was crazy, trying to get Frost and the others. Yes, I was crazy . . ."

His words trailed off as he reached for her hand, towing her up the garishly lighted slope, glimpsing her face. He saw the shock there, the look of betrayal, the revulsion at this second conviction.

He had the urge to turn back, to run down the hill and throw himself into the flames and perish there. But that would not make restitution. And before anything he must do his utmost to see these people to safety.

He did not know whether their escape from the burning hotel had been seen, and stopped to look back, to judge the chance of discovery. The fire, he thought, effectively had screened them this far, and as he looked the hotel building collapsed, twisting, falling inward, throwing a volcano of blazing debris and sparks high into the air. The buildings on either side had already exploded into flame and now the far side of the street, the boards heated to the point of ignition, the whole block caught.

There would be no stopping the holocaust. The entire town, as if cursed, would go. By morning only a river of smoking ashes and twisted metal would mark where the camp had climbed the gulch. The mob was now dispersed, racing for safety. He took a moment to wonder if they had saved the money wagons, if they could salvage at least that from this fiery ending of his cataclysm.

Then he turned again to the hill and the task ahead. He knew the mountain well, and the territory beyond it. Their best route lay in getting to the mine, then following the pipeline to the springs. From there it was still thirty miles to Goldfield over the rough road by which they had brought in the pipe.

He and Emma Bondford caught up with the group ahead as it paused to catch its breath. He let the moment run on and then said to Frost;

"Move on now, to the mine. We'll rest there through the day and head out when the moon gives us enough light."

But Amos Frost shook his head. "There'll be a crew at the mine."

Christian said sourly, "Not any longer, not after they saw the fire."

They climbed. María, with an animal strength, carried the little girl on her back, grasping at bushes to pull herself up step by step. Christian hoisted the boy to the saddle of his shoulders. They went up the long paw and around the knoll and came onto the shelf that had been leveled before the mine office. Here the moon laid a silver carpet on the open yard, unbroken except by their own long shadows.

Christian stopped and stood drawing air into his hard-used lungs, and Amos junior wriggled on his perch, his complaint proving that his confidence was restored.

"Mont, I'm hungry."

"You're out of luck," Christian told him. "There'll be no food here unless somebody left his lunch pail, but I think there'll be some coffee . . ."

He had raised his hands, closing them around the boy's trunk, beginning to lower him to his feet, and he was still speaking as the office door opened and Al Pierson stepped out, the barrel of his leveled rifle catching a glint of light. His teeth were bared in his wolflike grin. Two men came out behind him.

"I figured if you got away you'd head up here," Pierson gloated. "But you won't get clear again." He lifted the gun's nose.

Christian's tone was low, urgent. "Al, not here. The children."

A shot cut off the last of his words. Amos Frost's hand was in his pocket. He fired through the cloth. The bullet struck Pierson in the chest and knocked him back a step, into the man directly behind him. Instinctively the man caught Pierson, fumbling with his free hand for his side gun. Frost fired again, this time at the third man, who stumbled and went down.

But now the one who still held Pierson fired. Amos Frost sat down rather than fell. His knees bent and he sat slowly, his arms locked across his stomach, where he was hit, as if to hold himself together. Then he leaned forward, burying his face between his knees.

Christian, his hands still around the boy on his shoulders, made no move to reach for his holstered gun. He freed one hand and lifted it in a gesture of surrender.

The man facing him let go of Pierson's body and came forward cautiously, with the step of a stalking cat. Watching Christian's eyes, he extended his arm, reaching for the gun at Christian's belt. He did not see Amos Frost straighten behind him.

Mont Christian did see Frost, saw the painful slowness with which the wounded assayer drew the gun from his pocket, and knew that he could not prevent the shot. All he could do was take a slow sidewise step, to get the child on his shoulders as far as possible from the target, and pray that Frost's aim would not be too wild.

The move brought a sharp warning from his captor, then the man pitched forward as Frost shot him in the back.

Christian spun away, stooping to set the boy on the ground, and in the same motion reaching for his gun, but as he turned back he found the fallen man already dead.

He threw a quick look around, seeing that Emma Bondford had her back turned, hiding the little girl between herself and María, that Amos junior was crouched, poised to run, his eyes dark and huge, anchored on his father. Then Christian moved to Frost, who had again folded forward.

He bent and lifted the assayer as gently as he could and carried him into the office, straightening him as he laid him on the table. As he went to the wall to light the lamp in the bracket there, Emma Bondford appeared in the doorway, pale and silent. He tried to ease her tension with a smile.

"Tell María to take the children to the shaft house," he said.

She went in automatic obedience and Christian returned to Frost. The assayer was still alive, but when he had cut away the coat and shirt Christian knew that his old enemy would not live long. And there was nothing he could do. A doctor could not have healed that wound.

He left the office to drag the three bodies outside into the machine shop, where the children would not see them when they crossed the yard again. When he again went to the office he had two surprises. Emma Bondford stood beside the table, and Amos Frost was sitting up, his legs dangling over the edge, holding the girl's hands for balance.

Without raising his bowed head the man spoke, his voice dry with pain.

"Mont? Get me a pen . . . some paper . . . I haven't much time."

Christian angled off to the desk, found materials and the board to which the daily mine reports were fastened, guessing that it was a will Frost wanted to write. Where so lately he had wanted to strip this man of everything, to let him know utter ruin, he now hoped that the assayer had something left, something to help his children.

He came against the table and turned his back, using it as a support for the board, holding that over his shoulder, his fingertips keeping the paper in place. He felt the pressure as Frost wrote slowly, line after line, and then the stronger, triumphant flourish of the signature. Then Frost was saying,

"Emma, take this and sign it as my witness."

The girl took the board, but out of the caution that her father's lawyer had drummed into her, out of her long resentment of this man's tormenting her, she said;

"I can't sign it unless I read it."

"Sign it, damnit. It won't bite you. It's an order to my bankers to turn my accounts over to Christian and makes him guardian of the kids until they're twenty-one. There's plenty that wasn't in Snake Mountain."

Emma Bondford gasped and fought a battle with herself. Had no one else been involved she would not have spoken, but she could not risk the possibility of jeopardizing Peggy and young Amos.

"No," she said. "You must not trust your children to him. He is an escaped convict, from Yuma Penitentiary. He was sent there for murdering a man. His name isn't Christian. It's Gilbert Lorran."

Frost did not raise his head. He sat holding onto the edge of the table to stay upright. He said nothing for a long moment, and then a strange sound rose in his throat. Amos Frost was laughing, fighting a paroxysm of coughing that brought a rush of blood to his mouth. He leaned on one arm and used the other to wipe across his lips. He struggled to clear his throat, to be able to speak. At last he looked up, gray faced but clinging to life with a new surge of strength.

"Gil Lorran," he said. "Gil Lorran, come to Goldfield as a nemesis. Hunted me down. Set up Snake Mountain and sucked us all in. Because Hickman killed your Goldfield assayer and we framed you to get your mine. So you figured it out, and you got even. Ah, yes, you got even. So . . . so. Well, get me more paper. I'll straighten it out. I'll clear you."

Gilbert Lorran was unbelieving, doubting his ears. "You volunteer that, knowing that I got you all killed?"

Frost laughed again, in harsh, gibing mockery. "Not for you, Lorran, and it's no free gift to you. But you're the smartest man I ever met. I'm buying that smartness to take care of my kids. You can't do that if you're in Yuma."

CHAPTER
NINETEEN

Amos Frost died an hour later. He left the will which
Emma Bondford, still reluctant, signed as he watched.
He left the confession, more willingly witnessed by her
and by Lars Matson.

Matson had surprised them, riding up with a string
of trail horses, stopping to halloo in the yard. Christian,
intent on the play inside, did not hear him come, but
when the call came he moved cautiously to the door.
Ten minutes before, he would have stepped on through
the entrance, offering himself for whatever retaliation
would be demanded. Now he had a greater need than
he had ever had to stay alive.

He called back to Matson and watched the boy swing
down and come forward, his gun holstered, but his jaw
tight with determination. Short of the doorway he
stopped. In the early morning light he could not see
through the partly open entrance, and he called again.

"Miss Bondford and the kids in there with you? Are
they all right?"

"All right," said Christian. "Come in, Lars."

Matson stepped in, now embarrassed. He ignored
Christian, glanced at Frost and went directly to the girl.

"I'm sorry," he said. "I only wanted to round up that gang of looters and take them to Goldfield, to the law. I didn't expect the mob. Things got out of hand." He swung suddenly, drawing his gun, holding it on Frost and Christian.

"Mont" — the word was a cry — "I don't know why you did it; you made plenty of honest money, and I hate this, but I'm taking you two back."

Once again this day Mont Christian raised his hands, open palmed. "Emma," he said, "come and take my gun and give it to Lars. And Lars, you read these papers, then listen awhile. After that, see what you think."

Lars Matson read. He signed the confession when Frost insisted. He listened as Christian told his story, making no effort to excuse himself, accepting the full burden of his guilt. Finally the boy drew a deep and ragged breath.

"I'm sorry for you, Mont. It cost a lot. Dick Butler's dead. He came rushing out of the hotel with his clothes afire. Somebody shot him. But he was alive when I got to him, he told me to look for you, that you were trying to save Frost's family." The boy's eyes pleaded with the white-haired man in whom he had believed so deeply. "Mont, what do you mean to do now?"

Christian said levelly, "Take care of the children, if you'll let me."

Amos Frost, as if he had heard enough, straightened and lay back and was dead. Both Matson and Christian jumped at the first movement, easing him down to the table top. Then Christian, withdrawing his hands, stepped back.

"Also," he said, "I want to pay back all I can to the people of Snake Mountain. Was any of the money saved?"

"All that was in the wagons. They were all loaded and starting to move before we hit them."

"Good. With that and what I have in Nixon's bank and whatever Frost left there should be enough to pay the town."

"But you can't use Frost's money. That belongs to the kids."

"Does it?" Christian shook his head. "He made the first of it by stealing my Tombstone mine. The rest he got by buying stolen hi-grade. Is it still Frost's money?"

"What about the youngsters?" There was new pain in Lars Matson's eyes. "You're not going to abandon them?"

"I can work. I still know mining." Christian's mouth twisted in a wry smile. "With or without luck I can get a job somewhere, and I think they'll grow up just as happy with what I can give them. At least it will be clean."

The boy's face cleared and he sighed in relief. "I guess I'd like to go along with you." Then a new problem made him frown, and he was young enough that he could not hide his train of thought. He looked toward Emma Bondford, then back at Christian. "But they need a woman, don't they?"

Mont Christian turned to face the girl. "Emma, it isn't only the children who need you. With Yuma hanging over me, I couldn't speak before. But now . . . will you marry me?"

She flushed, looking at him directly, and started to speak. Then she stopped and her hands tightened into fists at her sides.

"I don't know . . ."

"I can't ask you to forgive what I've done, I know. That I will have to live with and try to make amends for. But I have learned. I will never again willingly bring grief to anyone."

She turned her head, looking through the door as if for escape. "Mont, wait. Give me a little time. I have to think through what I feel."

He did not press her. He motioned to Lars and they carried Frost's body out to the hillside. They dug four graves and when these were filled and covered they gathered the party and mounted the horses.

They did not go down the gulch. Though it was probably empty of people by now there was too much ugliness for them to want to look on it again. They turned out along the pipeline toward Goldfield.

CHAPTER
TWENTY

Word of the devastation of Snake Mountain ran ahead
of Mont Christian, carried by the first contingent of the
burned-out miners, and even Goldfield reacted with a
stunned shock. The story crossed the town like a prairie
fire. The name Christian changed swiftly from a
lodestone to a curse.

Late on the second night the white-haired man
picked a dark way into the town and sought out George
Nixon's house. There was no light, but he hammered at
the rear door until the banker opened it, dressed in his
nightclothes and a dressing robe. At sight of his visitor
he tried to close the door quickly, but Christian already
had it wedged and forced through the opening.

Nixon gave back only a step, standing his ground,
saying, "What the devil do you mean, coming here?"
He held the lighted oil lamp in his hand as if it were a
weapon.

"Half an hour is all I want," Christian said. "Just
listen to me. It's important."

Cold eyed, the banker watched him, barely nodding,
and again Christian went through his recital.

"I've sent the women and children on to Frost's
house," he said at last, "and I sent Lars Matson to

Prescott with the confession, to ask the Governor for a pardon. Now I want to ask you to act as trustee, of everything I have in your bank, of Frost's assets and of the money from the wagons. Use it all. First buy back the land that was bought around Snake Mountain, pay the building and business losses. Use whatever is left to buy up Snake Mountain stock on a pro rata basis."

"I would do it myself, but it will take Matson time to get back here, and until then I'll be a shooting duck. I can't afford to get myself killed now, with the children to look out for. I can't make a living for them if I'm not around. Will you do this?"

The banker listened, unbelieving at first, then skeptical, and finally accepted the story, for nothing was too improbable in Goldfield.

"Come into the study," he said. "Let's get it on paper. I don't want to wake up in the morning and find it was a dream."

Sitting at the desk, Christian gave him Frost's order on his banks, assigned his own funds and wrote an order, as last surviving officer of the Snake Mountain Company, for all assets that could be realized from it. Then, as he rose to leave, he added;

"There's one thing more. Will you tell the newspapers the full story?"

Nixon, relaxed at last, began to chuckle. "Try to keep me from it. The boys in this town need a little laugh right now. There are some who'll be feeling guilty about their part in the mob, and when the smoke blows down I think a good Saturday night brawl will account for about as much mayhem. I'd say you're paying your debt. But now, what are you going to do to keep alive?"

"I'll stay back in the hills until the paper comes out, until Matson has time to get back and clear me of the murder charge."

He left then, keeping in the shadows, making his way to the Frost house to tell Emma Bondford of his plans and ask her to stay with the children until his return. Then she would be free to leave, since apparently she could not bring herself to marry him.

As careful as he was, and without knowing it, he was seen and recognized. One man discovered him and ran to make the announcement in the nearest saloon. They started in a body, fanning through the area, working up toward the Frost house, and one of them saw his tall figure as it went through the lighted doorway. That one yelled and brought the others, perhaps a dozen, deploying them back and front to meet any attempted escape. Then they approached the house and shouted, demanding that Christian surrender.

Indoors, María stoically shrugged and began herding the children toward the upper floor, an indication that she thought he would as a matter of course fight. Christian did not stop her. He wanted one last moment with Emma Bondford. Then he would go out to them. He would make an effort to explain, but in the present temper of the town he doubted that anyone would listen to him again. When they had listened he had deceived them.

"Emma," he said, "the little package I gave you, to open in San Francisco, do you know where it is?"

Her eyes were wide, on the door. Beyond it the voices were growing impatient, and she had a vision of the violence at Snake Mountain being repeated here. She answered him without interest.

"It was in my bag, in the carriage. I don't know what happened to it."

He took her shoulders, turning her, forcing her to look at him. "Listen to me, Emma. The team ran away, probably out of town. Someone has probably found it and brought it in."

"In the morning try to locate it. There is money in the package, not a lot, but enough to get you started. Will you do one thing for me? Will you take the children and raise them?"

She stood looking at him, reading the meaning behind his words, and her breath drew in sharply.

"No," she said. "Oh, no . . ."

Then she had spun away from him and run to the door. Before he could catch her she had wrenched it open and darted onto the porch. He did not dare follow her for fear of drawing shots that might hit her, but he shouted his warning to the waiting crowd.

"Hold your fire. Don't shoot. I'm coming. Let her get clear."

"All right, all right. Come on where we can see you."

Christian stepped into the doorway and stood silhouetted against the light behind him, his hands hanging at his sides, a target that could not be missed.

But even as the outside voice answered him Emma Bondford was shouting, glancing back, moving to place

230

herself directly in front of Christian to shield him with her slight body.

"Wait . . . wait." Her voice was high with urgency, carrying across the wide street. "He's paying back everything you lost. You don't have to believe me. Go ask George Nixon. Oh, please, wait until the paper comes out. If you don't wait you will do a terrible thing."

She kept talking, jerkily, not always making sense. Because she was a woman, the men hesitated, drew back, undecided now. Then the leader called.

"Get out of the way, Ma'am. He's hoodwinked us long enough. Not even you can talk him out of this one . . ."

Behind her Christian said levelly, "Do as he says, Emma. Even dead I couldn't rest if you are hurt."

Instead of obeying, the eastern girl drew herself to her tallest, backed two steps until she stood against him and wrapped her arms behind her, around his waist.

"You'll have to kill me too," she called. "And if you kill either of us you will regret it all of your lives."

Christian could not risk moving to put her away. Any motion he made could trip a nervous finger on a trigger, could start guns blazing. He could only hold his breath and hope.

Below the porch the crowd leader lifted his hand, holding his gun, and scratched the side of his head with the muzzle. Then he turned around, facing his men, and pointed with the gun.

"You two boys, go get Nixon up, find out what she's talking about. The rest of us will wait here."

The two turned away, reluctant, but they went. The leader swung around again, relaxing. With Christian securely held under the guns of his fellows, curiosity rode up through him.

"You're Amos Frost's nursemaid, aren't you?" he said.

"I am the children's tutor." Emma Bondford's voice was strong, confident now that she had won their reason.

The man nodded. "You look like a lady. How can you stand up for the likes of this swindler?"

"Thank you for waiting," she said. "You will have your answer in a little while. But just at the moment, I don't want to be a widow before I'm a wife."

Goldfield always had loved a laugh. It loved the showy, the outrageous, the daring, and it had a reverence for this kind of woman.

The leader's mouth fell open. He turned slowly to look around his group. "By God," he said, "we called him right when we named him Lucky Christian."

In the doorway, Christian, still not daring to move his hands, leaned forward, leaned onto the girl and lowered his face into her hair. Against its scented warmth he whispered,

"Lucky Christian indeed. But I think we'll kill him off anyway. Emma, will you be Mrs. Gilbert Lorran?"

The girl tipped her head back, against his chest, and said in a voice that reached only him, "I will."

ISIS publish a wide range of books in large print, from fiction to biography. Any suggestions for books you would like to see in large print or audio are always welcome. Please send to the Editorial Department at:

ISIS Publishing Limited
7 Centremead
Osney Mead
Oxford OX2 0ES

A full list of titles is available free of charge from:

Ulverscroft Large Print Books Limited

(UK)
The Green
Bradgate Road, Anstey
Leicester LE7 7FU
Tel: (0116) 236 4325

(Australia)
P.O. Box 314
St Leonards
NSW 1590
Tel: (02) 9436 2622

(USA)
P.O. Box 1230
West Seneca
N.Y. 14224-1230
Tel: (716) 674 4270

(Canada)
P.O. Box 80038
Burlington
Ontario L7L 6B1
Tel: (905) 637 8734

(New Zealand)
P.O. Box 456
Feilding
Tel: (06) 323 6828

Details of **ISIS** complete and unabridged audio books are also available from these offices. Alternatively, contact your local library for details of their collection of **ISIS** large print and unabridged audio books.